Mottingham Library
0208 857 5406

https://capitadiscovery.co.uk/bromley

In partnership with

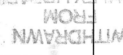

1 5 AUG 2016

THE LONDON BOROUGH
www.bromley.gov.uk

Please return/renew this item by the last date shown.
Books may also be renewed by phone and internet

D1078378

"**You could marry me.**"

Mirabella's mouth dropped open. She stared at Zane in absolute stunned silence. And then she shook her head, certain she had misheard him.

"I am really getting delusional," she half laughed. "For a second, I thought I heard you say you could marry you."

Zane moved in a little closer. Now that he'd said it out loud, it just seemed like it was the right solution. He didn't know why it had taken him this long to come up with it.

"You did. I did. You can."

She could only continue to stare at him in utter disbelief. "You're serious," she cried.

He didn't see the problem. Why was she having so much trouble accepting this? Had he been wrong about the attraction he thought was between them? "Why wouldn't I be?"

"Well, for one thing," she began to enumerate, "it's insane. For another, you don't love me."

Too late, Mirabella realized she hadn't phrased that properly. What she should have said was that they didn't love each other. But she had isolated it to just him who didn't love in this case. Had he picked up on the fact that she'd slipped, inadvertently letting him know how she felt about him?

* * *

We hope you enjoy this dramatic series:
The Coltons of Texas: Fighting love and buried family
secrets in the Lone Star State...

THE PREGNANT
COLTON BRIDE

BY
MARIE FERRARELLA

First Published in Great Britain 2016
By Mills & Boon, an imprint of HarperCollins*Publishers*
1 London Bridge Street, London, SE1 9GF

© 2016 by Harlequin Books S.A.

ISBN: 978-0-263-91941-7

18-0816

Special thanks and acknowledgement are given to Marie Ferrarella for her contribution to The Coltons of Texas series.

Printed and bound in Spain
by CPI, Barcelona

USA TODAY bestselling and RITA® Award-winning author **Marie Ferrarella** has written more than two-hundred-and-fifty books for Mills & Boon, some under the name Marie Nicole. Her romances are beloved by fans worldwide. Visit her website, www.marieferrarella.com.

To Daddy,
Who introduced me to
All those Western series on TV And
Sparked my love of the
Old West.
I miss you.

Prologue

He refused to believe it was true.

Eldridge Colton, the man who had adopted him, the only man he had ever really known as a father, had been kidnapped a month ago, and everyone now believed that the wealthy head of Colton Incorporated was dead.

But Zane Colton didn't. He refused to.

This, despite the fact that there'd been no ransom note, no mysterious caller, his or her voice effectively disguised thanks to modern technology to sound like some criminal in the witness protection program testifying in closed court. No one had even attempted to bargain, demanding a king's ransom in exchange for the wealthy, well-known Texas citizen's safe return.

Zane held fast to the fact that up until now there had been no body found. And even though there were a dozen explanations for that, until a body was discovered, he was going to continue believing that his stepfather was still alive.

Not just believing it, but actively doing something to find out what had happened to the man and where Eldridge had been all this time since the morning that Moira, the family housekeeper of long standing, had been dispatched to the patriarch's room because his wife, Whitney, had wanted him by her side as she attended another society breakfast.

Zane could still hear Moira's scream ringing in his ears. Moreover, he could hear his mother as she'd first railed indignantly at the housekeeper for making a scene, then dramatically dissolved into histrionics when Whitney had seen the blood on the bedroom floor and the windowsill. It was at that moment she had realized that her husband of almost thirty years was not just missing, but could quite possibly be dead.

Well, his mother might believe that, but Zane didn't. Oh, his stepfather was definitely missing—and had been for the past month, despite the presumably best efforts of Sheriff Troy Watkins and his two deputies. And since the blood in the bedroom had been tested and had turned out to be his stepfather's, he knew that Eldridge Colton was definitely hurt.

But dead? No, the man wasn't dead. Seventy-five-year-old, short, skinny Eldridge Colton was one tough SOB; he always had been. He couldn't be killed. Zane was certain that his gut would have told him otherwise if his stepfather was no longer among the living. The way he saw it, Eldridge had to be alive because he, Zane, hadn't really reached his own goal yet—to live up to what he felt were his stepfather's expectations of him.

Eldridge had married his mother when she was a widow with two very young children. At the time, Eldridge was a widower with two children of his own, Fowler and Alanna. The man hadn't had to adopt him and his sister, Marceline. He could have just as easily ignored them.

But he hadn't.

Instead, Eldridge had incorporated them into his life and, when the time had come, into his business— or at least he'd tried when it came to Marceline. But Marceline harbored her own ill will against Eldridge and refused to have him do anything for her that would place her into further debt to the man.

Eldridge had treated Zane well. He hadn't dictated to him like a despot whose word was law but had spoken to him like an understanding parent. When Zane had indicated to his stepfather that he was really very uncomfortable being a corporate suit in the grand scheme of things, Eldridge hadn't expressed disappointment, hadn't railed at him. Instead, his stepfather had made him his head of security for Colton Incorporated.

In his own way, the man had tried his best to be understanding when he really didn't have to be.

Eldridge Colton was a good, decent man, and Zane intended to find out just what had happened to him. He owed him that much. With luck—and Eldridge had once taught him that a man made his own luck— he was going to find the kidnapped CEO, and he was going to bring him back to his family.

Alive.

Chapter 1

She wasn't showing yet.

Despite the fact that she felt rounded and pudgy and could almost envision tiny, lightning bolt arrows coming in from 360 different directions, all conspicuously pointing at her stomach, Mirabella Freeman really wasn't showing yet.

But she knew it was just a matter of time before she would be.

So every morning, after she had showered and got dressed, Mirabella would look herself over very carefully in her wardrobe mirror from as many angles as she could manage. She was trying to reassure herself that her initially ironing-board-flat stomach still appeared that way.

Meanwhile, she did what she could to prepare for the inevitable. Though money had never been plentiful, she'd always known how to buy just the right pieces and make the most of the limited wardrobe she had. She'd always known how to divert attention away from what she felt to be her visible flaws. When she was very young, it had been her unruly red hair, so she had found a way to tame it and make the most of its good features.

Because her curves had come early—way earlier than the rest of the girls in her class—she had worn long blouses that gathered at her hip, diverting the eye there rather than at her rounded chest.

And now she was focused on making sure no one's attention was drawn to her waist, causing them to possibly suspect she was pregnant.

Society had evolved to the point that it really wasn't supposed to be a big deal for a single woman to be with child. But the people who ran Colton Incorporated were on the old-fashioned side and she didn't want to take any chances until she really had no other options but to let them know her condition.

Besides, with her hormones in an uproar the way they'd been lately, she was in no mood to be the subject of gossip and speculation even one second before she ultimately had to be.

As she craned her neck, looking over her shoulder into the wardrobe mirror from what amounted to a torturous angle, Mirabella silently lectured herself that she was being paranoid. How could she look pregnant when she'd actually *lost* weight in the last month? Some women suffered from morning sickness, especially with their first baby. She found herself suffering from *all day sickness.* No matter how hard she tried to avoid it, she was on her knees in front of the porcelain bowl several times a day, purging more often than a partying frat boy during his first year away from home. Everything, even water, seemed to make her miserably nauseous these days.

The hardest part, she thought as she slid into her shoes and picked up her purse, was trying not to let her boss, Zane Colton, find out about her frequent communing with the bathroom. Fortunately, the wickedly good-looking man still hadn't noticed.

She hoped to keep it that way.

As head of Colton Incorporated's security, it wasn't as if he was chained to his desk. The man clearly liked being on his feet and active, using any excuse to leave his office and get out both on the floor and into the field. He looked the most pensive and restless when necessity had him spending time at his desk, dealing with end of the month paperwork—even if that "paper" was on the computer.

But even with all the hours he spent away from his office, it was only a matter of time before he'd begin to notice just how often she was away from her own desk. Her desk was situated directly in front of his office, so, coming and going, the man couldn't miss seeing her—unless she wasn't there.

As far as bosses went, she thought, locking her front door, Zane was in a class by himself. Leaving aside the fact that the man was as good-looking as they came, with over half the women in the top two floors of the twenty-five-story glass office tower madly in love with him, Zane Colton was not a demanding boss. He was easygoing and completely devoid of an ego, even though he would have been more than justified having one.

He didn't act like a man who had anything to prove to anyone, except for possibly himself. And best of all, he didn't throw his weight around, the way some others did. She was extremely happy to be Zane Colton's administrative assistant and she wasn't about to jeopardize that for the world.

While she didn't *think* he would dismiss her if he discovered she was pregnant, it wasn't something she wanted to risk finding out, either.

Not until she absolutely had to, she decided with a huge sigh.

Besides, the man had something far more pressing and bigger to deal with than a pregnant employee who might not be able to perform her duties. As far as that went, she definitely was up to doing her job even in her present condition—but she had a feeling that what she said or didn't say carried very little weight at the moment.

But, be that as it may, something far bigger than the tiny seed growing within her had hit the corporation. Everybody, not just Zane, was still more or less reeling from shock. Zane's father, that nice old man who had started and owned the company, Eldridge Colton, had been kidnapped a little more than a month ago now and the sheriff still hadn't been able to find any trace of him.

Mirabella made no effort to suppress the shiver that zipped over her body as she thought about the current situation.

Some of the people she worked with believed Eldridge Colton was dead right from the beginning. Others felt he had been killed some time in the last couple of weeks.

Some people believed that, but not everybody.

From what she had overheard when Zane had been

talking to someone on the phone, her boss didn't belong to that group. Zane was utterly certain his father was still alive.

Or rather that his *step*father was still alive, Mirabella corrected herself.

But whatever label she affixed to Zane's relationship with the missing Mr. Colton, she knew her boss cared a great deal about the man and that he wasn't just going to passively wait for someone else to either stumble across the man's inert body or find him clinging to life somewhere, perhaps months from now. She knew Zane Colton intended to find the missing corporation founder *now*—or barring that, as close to now as he could possibly manage.

This was not a man who needed to hear his administrative assistant hesitantly ask for a moment of his time, timidly clear her throat and then nervously announce she was pregnant and throwing up her insides. Then quickly tell him not to worry, that she would find a way to incorporate her frequent dashes to the ladies' room into her workday so the latter wasn't adversely affected. She would then conclude by assuring him that all would work itself out for the best.

It was a phrase her grandmother used to frequently tell her when she was a little girl.

Her grandmother's wisdom not withstanding, Mirabella really didn't see how that was going to happen. It was hard to hold on to the little bit of optimism when her baby's father, after being informed of his pending fatherhood, had only four angry words to throw in her direction: *Get rid of it.*

He had been even less happy when she'd tersely held her ground and announced, *No.*

Feeling about as energetic as an overworked flea, Mirabella slid behind the steering wheel of her car and buckled up. She couldn't help wondering how long it would be before she had to adjust both her seat and her seat belt to accommodate her enlarged size.

She supposed there was a small, outside chance she wouldn't have to. There were, after all, some cases of women who had gone their entire pregnancy hardly gaining weight at all and never looking as though they were pregnant. Those cases were very few and far between, but they *did* happen.

But usually, in order for that to happen, she thought in the next moment as she started up her car, her baby would have to do only a minimum of growing in her womb—and something like that might wind up having dire consequences for the baby.

Just what kind of a vain monster was she? She couldn't wish for something like that, Mirabella upbraided herself.

No, she was a big girl who had done big girl things, Mirabella reminded herself, and now it was time to face up to the consequences. The little being inside of her wasn't going to be made to pay for her one wild, impetuous moment of irresponsibility.

That was on her.

Just not yet, Mirabella thought as she put her vehicle in Reverse and then pulled out of the parking spot.

Coward, the little voice in her head taunted.

Mirabella ignored the little voice. Lately, she'd gotten good at that.

When he had first begun to work at Colton Incorporated, each time he walked into the building, Zane used to feel as if all eyes were on him. He was certain that all the employees there, from the lowest to the board of directors surrounding his stepfather, were waiting for him to fall flat on his face and fail.

Fail big-time.

He didn't doubt that these other employees were convinced he was having everything handed to him—especially when Eldridge had promoted him to be the head of the company's security division. They hadn't known or realized, at least not at that point, that he'd had to prove himself. Prove himself to Eldridge and *especially* to himself. It wouldn't have meant something to him otherwise.

Eventually, he did prove himself.

But it had taken him time. Time to prove himself, to prove he was there to work, to get the job done and to resolve things as fairly as possible, making decisions to the best of his ability after listening to both sides of a problem. It hadn't been easy, but he'd done it.

In time, he'd dealt with everything from employee disputes, to embezzlement and to the ever challenging matter of internet security. He liked to feel that he did this all well. Eventually, he had his proof of that. People had begun to seek him out, to trust him to handle things fairly. To treat him with respect.

But that had all changed in the last month.

He was back to square one.

Lower than square one. Because now he couldn't help feeling that some of the employees were looking at him and wondering if he was somehow involved in his stepfather's disappearance.

He supposed in a way it made sense because, in reality, he was guilty of doing the very same thing each and every time he and his family gathered around the dining room table for a meal.

To the outside world, the various Colton siblings, as well as the woman who called herself their mother, did what they could to present a united front, to *appear* to have one another's backs. Privately, it was another story. It seemed as if they had always been at odds with one another, breaking up into smaller factions.

While Zane was always close to his younger sister, Marceline, she and Eldridge's oldest son, Fowler, used to go out of their way to make the three youngest Coltons, Thomas, Piper and Reid, miserable. And then there were times that the others would all gang up on Piper, a maid's daughter, who had been adopted by Eldridge and Whitney when her mother died.

As for himself, Zane had done his best to remain out of it all, focusing instead on just proving himself to the one man who mattered.

And now he was probably included in the mix of suspects, Zane couldn't help thinking. In these cases, the family was always the first to be suspected.

He stared at the blank screen on the computer monitor on his desk, his thoughts going in a dozen directions at once.

So far, no one had accused him of anything outright, but he had an uneasy feeling it was probably just a matter of time before that happened. Being the outsider was never something shaken off completely. The only way he could make sure he wasn't ever accused of such a heinous crime was to find Eldridge himself.

He had a far bigger stake in this than Sheriff Watkins did. After all, for him it was personal.

It wasn't for Watkins.

But how the hell did he go about finding his missing stepfather?

Zane felt as if he was going around in circles again, the way he had been ever since this whole thing had started.

If his father was dead, why hadn't whoever was responsible for this just killed him on the spot? Why take him and *then* kill him? It didn't make any actual sense.

And if his stepfather had been kidnapped for the usual reasons, where was the ransom note?

If he'd been taken for some other reason, as leverage or to be exchanged for something or someone, where was *that* call?

This whole thing wasn't adding up, Zane thought, frustrated. It was as if Eldridge had been taken for no reason.

He got up and began pacing around his desk, exasperation and impatience growing by the moment, feeling red-hot and ready to explode.

Zane struggled to hold on to his temper.

Giving in and taking it out on the first thing handy wasn't going to get him any closer to finding the only father he had ever known.

The best thing he could do for Eldridge—other than finding him, Zane thought ruefully—was to keep the company going in the man's absence. The company meant *everything* to the patriarch. This way, when he did come back, the company would be running smoothly instead of having devolved into a state of chaos.

Zane had been doing just that for the last month—keeping his end of the company going—but it was becoming harder and harder rather than easier.

With a sigh, he planted himself back behind his desk. He needed to get something productive done.

Distracted as he reviewed which department needed his attention the most this morning, he thought he heard a noise, but discounted it—

Until it came again.

It took him a moment to realize someone was knocking on the door. Bracing his palms against the edge of his desk, Zane took in a deep breath, then let it out slowly. He couldn't be seen losing his grip in front of the employees. Aside from something like that not inspiring confidence, it might very well be the thing which caused the better people around him to either look for another job—or circle his position like sharks, waiting for him to mess up.

Sorry, not about to do that. Not today, Zane promised. "Come in," he called out.

The door opened and Mirabella took a couple of steps across the office's threshold. One hand on the doorknob, she had her back up against the door. To Zane it looked as if she was trying to shrink or even disappear into the woodwork.

For just a split second, he found himself wondering about her, wondering what could cause a rather stunning woman like Mirabella to behave as if she was attempting to avoid the attention of the immediate world. Any other time or place, he would have taken an interest in the young woman, perhaps asked her a few detailed questions in order to get to the bottom of her unusual behavior.

But this wasn't any other time. It was *this* time, a time of impending crisis if his stepfather wasn't found.

For the umpteenth time, he made a solemn promise to himself to *find* the man.

Failure was not an option.

"Sheriff Watkins is here to see you, Mr. Colton," Mirabella informed him.

Instantly alert, Zane half rose behind his desk. "Send him in, Mirabella," he instructed.

The sheriff, a well-built, imposing man in his early fifties, took his time walking in. His gray eyes scanned the room, missing nothing. Polite, soft-spoken, he was nonetheless not a person to be trifled with.

A show of respect had Troy Watkins carrying his well-worn Stetson in his hand rather than wearing it. There were surprisingly few traces of gray in his dark hair, given the nature of his work combined with his age.

The expression on his sun-wrinkled face was stern, but then he'd never been known for smiling much. This morning was apparently no exception.

"Take a seat, Sheriff," Zane invited, gesturing toward the chair closest to his desk.

Watkins did so, but he looked as if he wasn't comfortable about it. Nor did he look as if he was comfortable in his present surroundings. He was a man most at ease when he was moving about in wide-open spaces. In his eyes, crowded cities were just necessary evils to be endured, not something to aspire to.

"What brings you here, Sheriff?" Zane asked, then immediately attached another, far more anxious question to the first one. "Did you find my father?"

"You mean your stepdaddy," Watkins corrected. "Gotta be accurate at all times, you know. If a man can't be accurate when it comes to the little details, it means that man's going to be careless when it comes to the big things."

He really wasn't in the mood for a lecture. What he wanted were answers. But snapping the sheriff's head off wouldn't get him anywhere. Zane tamped down his impatience and rephrased his question.

"Did you find my *step*father, Sheriff?"

"No," Watkins answered. He ran his fingers along the inside of his hat, turning the Stetson around in a slow circle. He raised his gray eyes to meet Zane's dark ones. "But I did find something interesting."

Chapter 2

Zane waited for the sheriff to continue, but obviously the man wanted to be coaxed.

Okay, Zane conceded. He was willing to play this game, just as long as it got him the answers he was after—and closer to finding out who had taken his stepfather.

"And what might that 'something interesting' be, Sheriff?" Zane asked.

Watkins slid a little more forward on his chair. As he did so, the man's small, gray eyes all but burrowed into him, seemingly taking full measure of him.

Elbows leaning on the armrests, the sheriff laced his fingers together in front of him as if he was relating a story around a campfire.

"Well, seems that your stepdaddy was making regular withdrawals from one of his private bank accounts, making them monthly to some bank account located heaven knows where—we haven't been able to track it down yet," Watkins continued, drawing out the revelation as he carefully watched Zane's face, apparently waiting for some telltale reaction. "Withdrawals to the tune of $9,999. That's the biggest amount he could have made without attracting the government's attention," Watkins added as if he were talking to someone who wasn't already aware of that fact. *Everyone* knew that little tidbit. Or at least everyone who was involved in finances and matters dealing with security, Zane thought impatiently.

Was the sheriff watching him for a reaction? Zane couldn't help wonder.

Well, he had a reaction all right. It was barely contained outrage.

He resented having this sprung on him out of nowhere, apparently for effect. "How long have you known this?" Zane wanted to know.

"Just today," Watkins answered mildly. The sheriff continued watching him the way a cat watched a mouse hole, breathless, waiting to pounce.

A few choice words rose to Zane's tongue, but he deliberately refrained from voicing any of them. It served no purpose telling the sheriff what he thought of his coming here, trying to bait him rather than being out in the field, looking for Eldridge.

Most of all, Zane was really growing tired of playing cat and mouse.

"Regular payments?" Zane questioned.

Watkins nodded his head. "Like clockwork."

Zane felt as if he was getting information out of the man by dribbles and drabs. "For how long?"

"Three months." Again, the gray eyes seemed to be burrowing right into him. "Why? What are you thinking?" he asked.

"Same thing you are," Zane answered vaguely.

It was a lie. He had a feeling, from the way Watkins was looking at him, that the sheriff was thinking a great many more things than just the one thing that had immediately struck him. Watkins might like presenting himself as being nothing more than a simple country sheriff, but under that easygoing exterior was a shrewd man, Zane decided. A man who didn't take kindly to being made to look foolish—and an unsolved crime of this magnitude, involving such a well-known citizen like Eldridge Colton, did just that.

Appearing to hang on his every word, Watkins cocked his head, looking right back at him, the very picture of innocence. "Which is?"

Why was Watkins waiting for him to spell it out? Was the man setting some sort of a trap for him, or was he just using him as a sounding board?

"Somebody was blackmailing my stepfather," he said, careful to use the sheriff-approved label for the man he considered his father. "Maybe the same person who kidnapped him."

Watkins scratched his head, as if that simple action helped him absorb the words a little better. "Now, why would he kidnap your stepdaddy if Mr. Colton was making regular payments to him?" Watkins asked.

Zane knew that Watkins knew the answer as well as he did, but again, he played along, answering the question as he wondered just exactly *what* the sheriff was really up to. In a nutshell, was the man trying to prove his innocence, or his guilt?

Or was he just casting about, hoping he—or who-ever else Watkins went on to question—would some-how trip themselves up and say the wrong thing?

He couldn't get a handle on it. All he knew was Watkins's rather clumsy method definitely made him feel uncomfortable.

Zane did his best to continue playing along, but his temper was really growing short. It had been this way ever since Eldridge had been taken.

"Maybe my stepfather got tired of paying the black-mailer. Or maybe the blackmailer had decided to up the ante and my stepfather said no. Or maybe," he speculated, coming up with a third reason, "whoever was blackmailing him just got too angry at my stepfa-ther and decided to take it out on him. I don't know," Zane snapped. "That's your job."

"Getting a mite testy, aren't you, son?" Watkins asked.

The man might be a couple of decades older than he was, but Zane wasn't about to stand being talked down to like this.

"I don't know. Am I?" he challenged. "What would you be like if it was your father who'd been kidnapped?"

"Stepfather," Watkins corrected, a little of his folksy cadence slipping away.

Zane had had just about enough of this. "How about we just call him Eldridge?" he proposed in an exas-perated tone. "Would that suit you?"

"Doesn't matter what suits me, Mr. Colton," Wat-kins replied calmly. "I'm just a lowly elected official of the county, trying to do his job." His eyes narrowed ever so slightly as they pinned Zane in place. "You wouldn't happen to know who was on the receiving end of these regular payments, now, would you?" he asked, his tone halfway between being solicitous and friendly.

"I haven't a clue," Zane responded tersely. And then he reversed the tables. "Do you?"

"Not yet," Watkins replied honestly. "But I aim to find out. You hear anything, Mr. Colton, I expect you to let me know," the sheriff said in a mild voice as he rose to his feet.

Zane knew he was being put on notice but he went out of his way to maintain a friendly tone. "Can I expect the same from you?"

Watkins inclined his head as if it was a wait-and-see situation.

"If I can," the sheriff replied.

Which translated to a big, fat *No*, Zane realized. The sheriff was not in the business of sharing. The only reason Watkins had come to him with this business of regular bank account withdrawals was to see his reaction to the news.

The sheriff was on a fishing expedition and he was looking to catch himself a big fish whose last name was Colton, Zane thought. He obviously believed that someone within the family had abducted Eldridge.

But why?

It wasn't as if there was a dearth of suspects outside of the family. Eldridge Colton had made his share of enemies in his youth.

Taking great pains to make sure none of his thoughts were registering on his face, Zane rose to his feet less than a beat after the sheriff had gained his. Then, rounding his desk, he walked the man to his office door.

"Thanks for stopping by, Sheriff," he said in the friendliest voice he could muster, "and for keeping me in the loop."

Watkins's eyes met his. Again, the sheriff's were unreadable. His lips spread just a little in what passed for a smile. An exceedingly shallow smile. "Count on it."

Zane felt as if he was once again being put on notice. This wasn't the first conversation he'd had with the sheriff, nor was it the first time he'd had the impression that Watkins would have been more than thrilled to pin this all on him—or at least on someone in his family.

All that meant, Zane thought as he shook the sheriff's hand and then watched the man walk away, was that he was going to have to get really serious about doing some intense investigating of his own.

His priorities converged with the sheriff's only insofar as wanting to solve the mystery of Eldridge's disappearance. Their paths diverged immediately after that because the sheriff suspected him while he, of course, knew he *wasn't* the one responsible for his father's disappearance.

He might have been at the house the morning of the abduction—they'd *all* been at the house that morning, it was everyone's customary starting point every Monday morning—but he hadn't gone anywhere near his father's room until *after* Moira had screamed because she'd found the blood.

He'd told Watkins as much, and the sheriff might have nodded when he heard that part, but Zane strongly suspected the man wasn't really convinced—

and wouldn't be until the real kidnapper was caught and confessed to the crime.

Until, Zane silently emphasized, not *if*.

Feeling momentarily overwhelmed, Zane suppressed a sigh.

"Is everything all right, Mr. Colton?"

Zane roused himself. Lost in thought, he hadn't realized he was still standing by his open door, staring after the departing sheriff, rather than going back to his desk.

"Not yet," he admitted, his voice a bit vague.

Looking at Mirabella, he flashed a quick smile in his administrative assistant's direction because she had expressed an interest in his well-being.

These days, a lot of people went out of their way to avoid him rather than be faced with having to find words of comfort and encouragement.

"But it will be," he concluded.

Mirabella pressed her lips together. Her stomach was suddenly rebelling again. Clenching one fist at her side, she struggled to exercise some sort of control over the queasy feeling. After all, she couldn't very well just dash off to the ladies' room in the middle of his sentence. Besides, Zane looked so lost for a moment, her heart went out to him.

"Was this about Mr. Eldridge?" she asked Zane quietly.

"Yes, it was," he replied.

Her eyes immediately widened and he caught himself thinking, despite the quagmire he found himself in, that her pale brown eyes looked beautiful.

Not the time, he admonished himself. *Besides, the*

woman works for you, you're not supposed to think of her that way.

A glimmer of fear had frozen on her face. "The sheriff didn't come to tell you…" She couldn't bring herself to finish the sentence.

She didn't need to. He could see Mirabella was thinking the worst. Zane immediately cut his assistant short, putting her mind at ease.

"No, he didn't," Zane told her. "It seems that there's just been another puzzle piece added to this mix."

"Oh." The single word escaped her lips, indicating she had no idea if this was good news or bad.

Mirabella wasn't asking him any questions and normally, he would have been grateful for that and wouldn't have volunteered anything. But today, this minute, filled to the brim with a host of tumultuous emotions, he found himself needing to *talk* to someone. His concern about his stepfather's ultimate welfare was eating away at him and he didn't know who to talk to, who to really trust.

There was something almost sweetly honest about the woman who quietly took care of all the myriad small details that went into making his job run as smoothly as it did.

In all the time they had worked together, there'd been no slipups. Mirabella was good at her job.

In the blink of an eye, she went from administrative assistant to temporary confidante.

"It's come to the sheriff's attention that someone might have been blackmailing my father," Zane told her without fanfare or hemming and hawing.

There was concern on Mirabella's delicate, heart-shaped face. Not a rush to judgment, not a quick, terse correction to remind him that Eldridge Colton was his stepfather, not his flesh-and-blood father.

Zane wasn't much of a talker, but he found Mirabella extremely easy to talk to. It was almost as if her very expression *coaxed* the words out of his mouth—and the weight off his shoulders.

"Blackmail?" she repeated in a small, hushed voice that almost vibrated with horrified disbelief. "Mr. Eldridge? Are you sure?"

Zane sighed, scrubbing his hand over his face. "Right now, Belle, I'm not sure of anything. But the sheriff came to tell me that one of my father's bank accounts was experiencing regular withdrawals once a month."

"Where were the withdrawals going?" Mirabella wanted to know. Who could be doing such an awful thing, blackmailing that sweet old man?

"That is what I intend to find out. Belle, get me—" He stopped talking and looked at her as if he hadn't really seen her today. "Are you feeling all right, Belle?" he asked.

No, I feel as if my stomach is being twisted inside out and it's all going to be coming up into my throat at any second, she thought, desperately trying to hold it together.

It was her own fault, she upbraided herself. She was the one asking questions, detaining Zane. She should have just nodded and withdrawn, pretending to go back to her desk. This way she could really be hurrying off to the ladies' room, praying it was unoccupied. The last thing she needed was to have someone overhearing her throwing up and offering to take her to the company nurse.

"I'm fine, sir," she told him, hoping she sounded convincing.

No, she wasn't, Zane observed. She wasn't fine. His administrative assistant looked very pale and it made him feel guilty. She was undoubtedly concerned about his father's well-being and reacting to what he'd just told her. Images of blackmailers and the way some might handle a situation that wasn't to their liking didn't exactly create calming scenarios.

He shouldn't have said anything to her.

Feeling responsible for making her feel this way, Zane took her hand in his in a gesture of comfort.

"Don't worry," he assured her, "he'll be all right."

Mirabella looked at her boss, confused even as she found herself reacting to the gentle way he was holding her hand.

There'd never been any physical contact between them before. Despite the nausea gripping her, something else was going on as well, something faint, but compelling nonetheless. She had no idea where this was coming from or why it seemed to momentarily supersede everything else.

This assault on her hormones she experienced because of the baby had literally knocked out all the rules. She quite frankly didn't know what to expect from herself from one minute to the next.

Right now, all she could think about was telling Zane how totally attracted to him she was. It was a real struggle not to. Almost as much of a struggle as it was to keep down whatever was threatening to purge itself right this minute.

So she forced herself to smile, desperately hoping

she wasn't going to start sweating—which she knew would only lead to more questions.

Instead, she said, "I know everything will be all right because you'll find Mr. Eldridge, I know you will."

"First thing I'm going to find," Zane told her, releasing her hand and turning toward his desk, "is exactly where and to whom these monthly withdrawals are going."

Though everything within her screamed to leave right this second while she still could, before risking embarrassment, Mirabella had to ask, "The sheriff really didn't tell you?"

"The sheriff indicated he didn't know." Whether or not that was the truth he didn't know, but he was going with that assumption for now. "He said something about it going into an untraceable bank account."

Which could very well be the truth. Despite the fact that this was the age of the hacker and people who were versed in all sorts of internet sleight of hand, not everyone was a cyber expert.

Be that as it may, Zane had the feeling the sheriff was not the country bumpkin he wanted everyone to believe him to be. That was just to throw everyone off their game and cause them to let slip things they might not have around someone they considered to be more savvy.

Whatever the case, right now he didn't have the time to spend trying to figure the sheriff out. He needed to track down exactly where Eldridge's withdrawals were going and just who was on the receiving end of those withdrawals.

And just as important, he needed to find out why. Just what was his father being blackmailed about?

"Will there be anything else, Mr. Colton?" Mirabella asked, really struggling not to allow her breakfast to come up.

"No, not right now," he replied, looking away. And then he looked up again. "Wait," he called after her.

Her back now to him, Mirabella didn't turn around. Instead, she pressed her hand against her chest. She was going to start heaving any second.

A rather breathless "Yes?" was really all she could manage in the way of a reply.

"Get me Meyer Stanley on the phone," he requested, addressing the words to her back.

Meyer was his recently transferred IT wizard, the man who could track down absolutely anything via the internet. If Meyer couldn't find something, then it didn't exist.

Mirabella remained where she was, with her back still facing him. Rather than turning around or even verbally responding to the request, Mirabella merely nodded her head and then held up one hand in the air, jiggling it as if to confirm she had heard him and she would get the man's number immediately.

Then, before he could say anything further—or had a chance to inquire after her health again because she was behaving so oddly—Mirabella all but fled the room, pulling the door closed behind her.

Leaving Zane to stare at it in utter, albeit fleeting, bewilderment.

The next moment his mind was back on his stepfather and the mysterious monthly withdrawals. Things were becoming much more complicated.

Just what the hell was going on here?

Chapter 3

His IT wizard still hadn't gotten back to him, but then, Meyer had only been given the assignment a little more than a day ago, Zane reminded himself. Even wizardry took time.

He took comfort in the fact that nothing was ever totally untraceable. Tracking something down through cyberspace wasn't impossible, just exceedingly time-consuming and tricky, requiring a great deal of patience, especially if they were dealing with an expert. He would be the first to admit that.

Even so, a restlessness was threatening to completely undo Zane if he didn't get out of the office for at least a little while and hit the field himself. If, in the interim, Meyer came up with anything, the man knew enough to make sure to reach him on his cell phone. These days it felt as if his phone was another appendage, never out of reach.

As he walked out of his office, habit had Zane glancing at Mirabella's desk.

She wasn't there.

Lately, whenever he passed her desk, either on his way in or out of his office, he'd noticed that more than half the time, the woman wasn't at her desk. *Was* she ill the way he'd suspected yesterday?

Pausing for a moment, Zane tried to remember if he'd heard anything about a bug going around the office lately, but came up empty. If he were being totally honest with himself, he was rather oblivious to common everyday occurrences lately. Everything in life as he normally knew it had taken a distant backseat to his stepfather's disappearance.

Even so, bug or not, the next time their paths crossed, he was going to confront Mirabella about his suspicions again, and this time he wasn't going to allow her to just shrug them off. He both appreciated and understood the woman's dedication to her job, but he didn't want her coming in if she was feeling ill. There was such a thing as carrying dedication too far.

Maybe he should pay attention to his own philosophy, Zane silently lectured himself. Investigations belonged in the hands of investigators, not in the hands of relatives who were too close to the situation to be impartial detectives.

That might be true, he wordlessly granted the next moment, but who had the bigger stake in finding his father, some worn-out sheriff or someone who cared whether or not Eldridge Colton lived or died? Zane knew the answer to that.

Turning down the hall, he was on his way to the elevator when he caught a glimpse of Mirabella emerging from the ladies' room. To his recollection she was looking even paler than she had earlier this morning which was an ash-gray theme and variation on how pale she'd appeared yesterday.

As she approached, he saw his administrative assistant was wiping her forehead with the wadded up handkerchief she had in her hand.

For a split second, he thought of just giving Mirabella her privacy and merely nodding as he passed, telling her that he was planning on being out of the office for the next hour or so.

But, although Zane believed in allotting people their own space, he *didn't* believe in avoiding situations— even if they were awkward—not if those situations needed to be dealt with.

And this one, in his opinion, obviously did.

So rather than keep on walking, Zane made a point of stopping directly in front of his administrative assistant, a six-foot-three-inch roadblock that was bent on keeping her from returning to her desk until he'd gotten a few answers.

Placing his hands on either side of her shoulders, Zane looked directly into her eyes and voiced his concern without beating around the bush.

"Tell me the truth, Belle. Were you just in there—" he nodded toward the ladies' room "—being sick?"

For a second, Mirabella stopped breathing. Oh Lord, did he suspect? She'd been so careful to keep her retching as quiet as possible, afraid anyone coming into the ladies' room might overhear her and put two and two together. From there it was only a very short leap to the status of office gossip.

Her mind raced to come up with a plausible response. Feeling weak and unsteady on her legs, not to mention feeling as if she'd thrown up the entire meager contents of her wretched stomach, going all the way back to yesterday's breakfast, Mirabella did her best to look as if she had absolutely no idea what her boss was talking about.

She assumed a mystified expression. "What do you mean by 'sick'?"

"Sick," Zane repeated, as if saying the word with emphasis somehow made it clearer for her. "You know, feverish, under the weather, maybe even sweating." He deliberately looked at the wadded-up handkerchief in her hand, then added, "And throwing up."

Her eyes instantly widened. "I haven't been throwing up," she denied so quickly he could almost feel the breeze created by her words.

"Okay, I believe you," he said in a calming voice, although, to be honest, he really *didn't* believe her. "It's just that while I really appreciate your dedication and having someone I can rely on, that *someone* isn't going to do me any good if she's going to wind up working herself into a hospital bed—or worse," he told her. His eyes held Mirabella's as he went on to ask, "Am I making myself understood?"

Mirabella pressed her lips together, struggling to look as if everything was all right instead of in a state of almost complete upheaval. "Yes, sir."

She looked like the picture of innocence, but he had a feeling he really wasn't getting through to her. He'd never met a redheaded woman yet who, politely or not, wasn't stubborn beyond words.

Still, he pressed on. "And if you need to go home

and go to bed in order to get better, I want you to go do just that."

Going to bed was what got me into this situation to begin with, Mirabella couldn't help thinking ruefully.

Out loud, she told Zane, "That's very kind of you, Mr. Colton, but I'm fine."

"Belle," Zane began, hesitating for a moment before finally continuing, "forgive me for being blunt here, but you really don't look fine."

She looked away and shrugged. "Bad hair day," she murmured.

"Your hair is beautiful as always," Zane said like a man who had no idea he was paying a woman a compliment instead of just simply stating what to him was an obvious fact. "Your face, however looks really pale."

She became a tad defensive when she heard that. "I'm a redhead, it comes with the territory," she said, wishing he would stop being so nice and just walk away like any normal, self-absorbed boss.

But he wasn't a normal, self-absorbed boss, which was why, despite her best efforts not to, she found herself being so strongly attracted to him.

"I'm aware of that," Zane replied patiently. "But you're looking paler than usual."

Mirabella blinked, totally surprised. "You've noticed how pale I am?" she asked, not knowing whether to be pleased because what Zane had just said meant he was paying attention to her, or insulted because his assessment was less than flattering—even if it was undoubtedly true.

Maybe he hadn't worded that quite right, Zane realized. Still, it was out and he needed to do a little damage control.

"You're a difficult person to ignore, Belle," he told her, sounding as formal as he could. "Now if you're feeling sick, say so and go home. There's nothing here that can't wait for a few days."

This isn't going to go away in a few days. It's not going to go away for another six months, she told him silently.

Stubbornly, Mirabella shook her head in response to his instructions. "I don't need to go home. It's just something I ate," she assured him with as much feeling as she could feign. "I'm over the worst of it. Now if you'll excuse me, I've got to get back to my desk. I have those notes of yours to input."

He looked at her dubiously. He knew she was lying about feeling better, but short of throwing her over his shoulder, carrying her to his car and driving her home, there wasn't anything he could do. If he tried to force her to do what he'd just instructed her to do, it might even be viewed as harassment by some and the last thing he needed at a time like this was to get embroiled in a case involving acts of harassment.

With no other option opened to him, Zane merely nodded and told her, "I'll see you in about an hour." He turned away, intent on heading toward the elevator banks.

He took exactly three steps in that direction when he saw the elevator door on the far end opening and the sheriff emerging with one of his deputies, Charlie Kidwell, right behind him. Both men appeared to look rather grim—and they were both looking at him.

Zane froze in place.

The sheriff was paying him two visits in the space of two days. This couldn't be good, he couldn't help thinking.

How did a man brace himself to hear news he didn't want to hear?

Zane had no answer for that. All he could do was fervently hope he was wrong about the sheriff's reason for this second visit.

"You're back, Sheriff," Zane said by way of a greeting to the older man. His voice sounded stilted to his own ears, but it was all he could come up with at the spur of the moment.

"Looks like it," Watkins acknowledged, his face devoid of any expression.

Zane's mouth felt like cotton.

He was really trying to prolong this process, as though the message the sheriff was bringing would somehow change if he stalled long enough. "You were just here yesterday. Mind if I ask what you're doing back here so soon?"

"I don't mind," Watkins assured him.

Zane had the distinct impression he was being toyed with and it helped him to rally. If the sheriff was toying with him, then the news couldn't be bad, right? Or could it?

"As a matter of fact," the sheriff drawled, "I'm going to tell you right now what made me come back so soon. You see, while going over the outside of the crime scene earlier today, I found this here little thing in the bushes that the other fellas from the crime scene unit must have missed the first time around."

Zane had a strange, sinking feeling he wasn't

going to like the answer, but he had to ask. "What little thing?"

Watkins smiled broadly. It was a humorless smile that still seemed to smack of satisfaction.

"Glad you asked. It was a cuff link. Now, I don't have any myself. I'm just a regular old-buttons-on-my-shirts kind of guy. But you rich fellas, you like all that pretty extra stuff," Watkins said, glancing at his deputy as if waiting for the other man to agree. But before Kidwell could say anything, Watkins continued. "Problem with cuff links and things of that nature, is that sometimes, you lose 'em and don't even know it. Which must be how you lost yours," Watkins concluded, holding up the cuff link, which was in a see-through evidence bag—as if it was exhibit A.

Zane frowned. Was this where the sheriff's dance finally led? His eyes narrowed as he glared at the older man. "Are you saying you found my cuff link near the crime scene?"

Watkins smiled again. "That's what I'm saying. Can't put nothing over on you, can I?" the sheriff asked sarcastically. Dropping at least part of his warm, friendly act, Watkins told him, "I'd like you to come with me so we can have a little conversation about that cuff link and how it happened to be where it was found."

Zane stared at the sheriff, stunned. Out of the corner of his eye, he could see Mirabella was having the exact same reaction as he was to what the sheriff was implying.

"Are you arresting me, Sheriff?" he asked in disbelief.

"No, not yet anyway," he said mildly. And then, in a far less innocent tone of voice he asked, "Should I be?"

"No, you shouldn't be," Zane said with feeling. "I didn't kidnap my fa— Eldridge," he corrected himself, not wanting to have to listen to the sheriff do it. "You *know* that."

"Right now, Mr. Colton, I don't know very much of anything," Watkins told him. "Except that Eldridge Colton is missing and nobody's found hide nor hair of him. Which just has me scratching my head and trying my damndest to put all the little pieces together." His eyes shifted to Zane's face, assuming a sterner expression. "What I'd appreciate is having you come down to the station with me so we can have ourselves a little conversation about how that cuff link of yours just *happened* to find itself in the bushes outside your stepdaddy's window." The fake smile was back as he added, "It couldn't have just walked there all by itself."

"There's a simple explanation for that," Zane began. He definitely didn't like what the sheriff was all but flatly stating.

With exaggerated politeness, the sheriff cut him off. "And I am looking forward to hearing that simple explanation—right after I get you to the station. Now, you can either come peacefully, or I can slap the cuffs on you and take you into custody in front of all those nice people in this building. It don't make no matter to me one way or the other, but I suspect it does to you, Mr. Colton. So I leave it all up to you. The choice is yours."

"I'll come peacefully," Zane answered through clenched teeth, feeling as far from peaceful as humanly possible.

Watkins pushed his Stetson back with the tip of

his thumb. "Good choice," he agreed with exaggerated approval.

Mirabella had been standing by silently all this time. But seeing the sheriff put his hand on Zane's elbow just now, as if he was about to usher him into the elevator, she suddenly snapped to life.

Moving as quickly as she could, she placed herself in front of the elevator door, barring entrance into the elevator car once it arrived.

"You'd best step out of the way if you know what's good for you, little lady," Watkins advised. His tone might have seemed exceedingly friendly, but the look in his eyes held a warning.

Mirabella took no notice. Her attention was entirely focused on Zane. "Do you want me to call the corporate lawyers, Mr. Colton?" she asked, deliberately ignoring the sheriff and his deputy. "Or your personal lawyer?" she suggested in the next breath. She thought that might be the best thing to do, given the way the sheriff was behaving toward Zane.

"No, not yet, Belle," Zane answered. "I don't need a lawyer."

Mirabella tended to disagree. She looked at Zane, worried in addition to feeling sick to her stomach. She knew in her heart that Zane couldn't have harmed Eldridge in any way, which was more than she could say about some members of the Colton family, who would do anything to advance themselves. But what she thought didn't matter. And to an outsider, it appeared that Zane really could use some legal counsel.

Especially when the sheriff asked in a voice that bespoke of impending doom. "You sure about that,

Mr. Colton? Having your lawyer there might prove to be very…handy," Watkins finally concluded.

"I've got nothing to prove and nothing to hide," Zane stated flatly. "So, no, I don't need to have a lawyer present." His eyes shifted to Watkins. "But thank you for your concern, Sheriff," he added coldly.

Watkins merely shrugged indifferently. "Suit yourself, Mr. Colton, but I'm going on record as saying I think you're making a big mistake not having this little lady get you that lawyer of yours." His gray eyes shifted toward Mirabella. "And you're my witness, little lady," he said, emphasizing this fact.

Mirabella clenched her hands into fists, but kept them firmly against her sides. She knew she was expected to keep silent, to just be part of the decor, but she couldn't in all good conscience say nothing.

"What I'm a witness to, Sheriff Watkins, is one of your bigger mistakes. Mr. Colton didn't kidnap or harm Mr. Eldridge," she told him fiercely. "He wouldn't do something so awful."

Ordinarily, Watkins would have just ignored her the way he ignored mosquitoes unless they had the misfortune of landing on him. However, he was amused by her bravado. So, the sheriff paused and looked at her.

"And you know this because…"

Mirabella drew herself up to her full height. "Because I have—and use—the common sense the good Lord gave me. Something that you, Sheriff, are apparently lacking."

Zane had no idea exactly what the sheriff might be capable of if pushed too far. And, in any event, he didn't want Mirabella drawn into this. There was just something about her that brought out the protector in him.

"Belle, don't," he instructed firmly. "It's going to be all right. You just hold down the fort until I get back."

She squared her shoulders, resigned, but not defeated. "All right, but I still think you should let me call the lawyer."

A faint bell dinged, announcing the elevator had arrived.

"Smart girl. You should listen to her," Watkins advised as he ushered Zane into the elevator car. The deputy got on behind them.

"Maybe later," Zane retorted.

"Suit yourself. But later might be too late," the sheriff predicted.

Mirabella's heart sank as she watched the elevator doors close, cutting off her view of Zane.

She had a bad feeling about this.

Chapter 4

Watkins silently walked into the small area that doubled as an interrogation room when it wasn't being used as a break room by his deputies. Zane had been sitting there for the better part of an hour, waiting for the sheriff to return after he had placed him there, telling him to wait and that he would be back soon.

Obviously they had different definitions of the word *soon*, Zane thought. But then, he was aware Watkins was toying with him.

Entering from behind Zane, the sheriff dropped a sealed evidence bag on the table right in front of him. The contents of the bag made a small "ping" noise as it made contact with the metal tabletop.

"Now, then," Watkins declared, "I believe that there is your cuff link, Mr. Colton. You're not going to waste your breath and my time denying it, are you?" he challenged, sitting down opposite Zane. "What with those pretty initials on it and all, saying Z.C., I figure that cuff link's gotta be yours."

Zane looked at the item in question. Even contained in the see-through evidence bag the way it was, the cuff link managed to catch the room's overhead light. It gleamed almost defiantly as it lay there in the center of the small metal table.

Zane raised his eyes to look at the smug expression on the sheriff's face. He could see Watkins was just itching for him to deny ownership. The sheriff was a man who relished fighting—and enjoyed winning.

He was not about to give Watkins that satisfaction.

"It's mine," Zane replied.

He'd only noticed that the cuff link was missing sometime toward the latter part of the day that his father had been presumably kidnapped. With bigger things to deal with than a missing cuff link, he hadn't even tried to find it.

Apparently Watkins had.

"Well, I'm glad we got that out of the way," Watkins said, referring to his suspect's admission. "Now, just what was it doing in the bushes right outside your step-daddy's window?" Watkins asked in a faux friendly voice, his eyes once again all but pinning Zane to his seat.

Watkins was the kind of man he could easily lose his temper with, but Zane knew he only stood to lose if he did so. Exercising total restraint, he managed to control his temper. He only sounded mildly sarcastic as he answered the sheriff's question.

"I don't know, I must have lost it while I was out there, looking for Eldridge after we discovered he wasn't in his room and we found his blood all over the floor."

Watkins's expression remained skeptical. "Or maybe you lost it while dragging your stepfather's body out through his bedroom window. If you ask me, that seems more logical," Watkins deliberately concluded.

Aggravated, Zane bit back a few choice retorts. Instead, he said evenly, "I was in an entirely different section of the house when my *step*father was taken."

Watkins asked dubiously, "Can anyone verify that?"

Zane met the man's eyes without any hesitation. "I was with my mother."

"Your mother," Watkins repeated with a smirk. "Sure you want to go with that?"

"Why shouldn't I?" Zane fired back. "It is the truth."

Watkins's short laugh told him what the sheriff thought of his alibi. "Well, throughout history, a lot of mamas have been known to lie for their sons. For instance, the mamas who were the wives of rich, powerful men. They often just looked the other way when their sons rid them of those men." Watkins leaned closer over the table as if he were sharing some sort of deep, dark confidence. "You take that Emperor Nero's mama as an example. Did you know Nero's mama poisoned her husband so her boy Nero could become emperor?" Watkins asked, chuckling as he spoke.

For two cents, Zane would have been more than willing to tell the sheriff exactly what he thought of the man, but he knew it would do him no good, only harm. Zane was determined not to allow the man to goad him into losing his temper.

"Fascinating as that is, Sheriff," Zane told him, "I do have another witness."

The hell you do, boy.

Watkins clearly didn't believe him as he asked, "And this witness just happened to conveniently pop up in your memory now?"

Zane ignored the sheriff's mocking tone and continued telling him his alibi. "The family housekeeper, Moira, was there at the time, as well. You might recall the name, Sheriff. Moira was the first one to discover my father was missing after my mother had sent her to the master suite to wake him up. It was Moira's screams that alerted everyone else to the crime." And then Zane restated his location. "I was nowhere near that side of the house when my father was taken."

Unfazed, the sheriff continued with his accusation. "You could have taken him earlier."

Watkins wasn't letting up. Zane was now convinced the sheriff was just trying to bait him and get him rattled. Rattled people said all sorts of incriminating things.

Zane continued to maintain his innocence.

"There was evidence that my stepfather fought his kidnapper. The room looked like a hurricane had hit it." And then he homed in on the main thing that would back up his claim. "One of the things knocked over in the struggle was an heirloom clock. Its face was smashed and the time on it stopped at 7:30." He remembered his sister pointing that out at the time. "At 7:30 I was sitting in the dining room, having coffee with my mother."

Watkins made a dismissive noise. "That's a nice little story."

All right, he'd been polite. He'd been patient. But enough was enough, Zane thought. He wasn't about to be bullied or browbeaten by Watkins any longer. The sheriff had fixated on him long enough. The man needed to turn his attention to catching the real kidnapper, not sit around, spinning fairy tales because it suited his purposes.

"Do you have any real evidence linking me to my stepfather's disappearance, other than a cuff link I could have easily lost at *any* time?" Zane demanded. When Watkins made no response, other than to glare at him begrudgingly, Zane nodded his head in satisfaction. "I didn't think so."

Rising from his chair, he declared, "We're done here. Sheriff."

"For now," Watkins allowed as he got up, as well. "But I'll be in touch."

"I'm sure you will," Zane snorted.

"Charlie," Watkins called out to his deputy. "Take Mr. Colton back to his office."

Zane was quick to cancel the order. He just wanted to leave all three officers of the law behind him. "Don't bother, Charlie," he said. "I'll find my own way back."

He didn't like being countermanded, but to save face Watkins shrugged indifferently. "Suit yourself, Mr. Colton. Have a nice day," he called after Zane.

Zane didn't bother turning around or even acknowledging he had heard the sheriff's sarcastic parting words.

Zane suppressed a sigh. He was in the clear for now, but he knew it would be just a matter of time before the sheriff came up with something else that would help him point a finger at one of the Coltons again.

Although theirs was the most prominent family living in the area, that didn't keep some people from viewing his family in a vindictive, jealous light. Those were the people who would be willing to do anything to tear the Coltons down in the public's eyes.

Watkins either belonged to that group, or to the group determined to show everyone that they were not influenced by the Coltons and would do whatever it took to bring one of them to so-called justice. Apparently the little matter of first being found guilty by a jury of their peers had mysteriously fallen by the wayside.

Zane blew out a breath. There was no point in making himself crazy over this. There was another way to deal with it.

Once outside the sheriff's station, Zane took out his cell phone and put in a call to his office. It rang a total of five times before the receiver was finally picked up.

"Mr. Zane Colton's office. How may I help you?"

Zane unconsciously smiled to himself. There was no mistaking that voice.

Mirabella tried not to sound breathless. She'd just gotten back from the ladies' room and had nearly been too late to pick up the line. She'd run to her phone. After five rings, the call would have gone to voice mail.

"You can pick me up and get me the hell out of here."

Relief did a quick sashay through her before Mirabella could think to block it. "Zane?" she cried happily. Belatedly, she realized she'd addressed him far too personally, given her position. She quickly cleared her throat and said, "I mean, Mr. Colton, is that you?"

"Yes, Belle, it's me." Zane looked over his shoulder, half expecting the sheriff to emerge from the office and ask him to come back under some new pretext. "And I need you to bring my car down here and pick me up."

All sorts of things were going through her head, more than half of them having to do with fugitives fleeing the law. Her breathing grew more rapid as her concern escalated.

"Where are you, sir?"

"Right now, I'm standing in front of the sheriff's office," he told her. "And I'd really rather not spend any more time doing that than I absolutely have to. The man is out for blood. It doesn't matter whose."

But Mirabella was still focused on the first part of his statement.

"They let you go?" she cried.

"They had nothing to hold me on," Zane informed her, surprisingly touched by the concern he heard in her voice. "I told you not to worry," he reminded her. "I didn't need our lawyer, after all."

Her sigh of relief was audible over the phone. "I should have realized you'd make them see reason, Mr. Colton."

He didn't need to be flattered. What he needed was to be picked up.

"How soon do you think you can get here?" He wanted to know.

"I'm already on my way to the elevator," she answered, which was stretching the truth since she'd taken the call on the office phone and was thus forced to stand there until she terminated the call. "I'll be there as soon as I can."

"Don't commit any traffic violations," he warned. "I don't want you arrested for speeding or going through a red light." He warily glanced toward the sheriff's office again. No one was coming out. "I'm not exactly friends with the sheriff around here."

"Understood. Speed limit all the way," she promised. "I'll see you soon."

"Can't be soon enough for me," Zane commented as he hung up.

Mirabella's heart jumped as she hurried out of the office and toward the elevator. She knew Zane was referring to the fact that he wanted to get away from the sheriff, the man's department and his office, but just for the space of a moment, she isolated Zane's last sentence and pretended the words had a completely different meaning, a different intent behind them. Specifically, that he was eager to see her, not just eager to be taken away from the sheriff's presence.

If only…

True to her word, Mirabella got there as quickly as humanly possible while still abiding by—for the most part—the speed limit. The way his face lit up when she turned the corner and first came into his view would have been well worth any amount of traffic tickets in exchange.

She came to a full stop at the curb. Her relief over Zane not being arrested was so huge, it was all she could do to restrain herself from jumping out and giving Zane a heartfelt hug.

Knowing she couldn't overstep her boundaries, Mirabella did her best to appear calm and collected. She waited until he opened the passenger door before asking, "Then everything's all right?"

"Oh, it's far from all right," Zane responded as

he dropped into the passenger seat. Then, before she could ask any further questions, he explained. "My father's still missing and presumed dead by some. And even though Watkins was forced to let me go right now for lack of evidence, it's just a matter of time before the good sheriff is back at it, not carrying on a proper investigation and trying to pin my father's kidnapping on either me or someone else in the family."

Mirabella knew all that was required of her was silence. That and a ride back to the office. But she just couldn't keep quiet, not when she looked at him and saw what he was going through.

"What are you going to do?" she finally asked him, watching a cavalcade of emotions parade across Zane's rugged face.

"Same thing I was going to do before the sheriff decided to accuse me of kidnapping and whisked me off to that poor excuse of an interrogation room. I'm going to find out exactly what happened to my father and who's responsible for it." He thought about the assignment he'd given to his IT expert. "I've got a lead Meyer Stanley is following up on. Hopefully, he's made some headway and will get back to me soon."

Taking in every syllable as if it was golden, Mirabella nodded. "And until then?"

Zane sighed, resigned to playing a waiting game for the time being.

"And until then, we'll keep my father's company running as smoothly as we can, getting things done that need doing. When he comes back, I don't want my father returning to a corporation that's falling apart or on the verge of bankruptcy, or a takeover. Or some kind of trumped-up investigation."

At this point, until he knew who he was dealing with, he wouldn't think of anything as unapproachable or safe. "I want him coming back to a business that's doing even better than it was when he suddenly disappeared."

Mirabella smiled at him as she came to a stop at a red light. "I hope you know Mr. Eldridge is very lucky to have you."

"It works both ways, Belle," Zane told her. "My sister and I are lucky to have him. A lot of men in Eldridge Colton's position would have kicked their wives' first kids to the curb, or exiled them to a year-round program at some boarding school the second they were old enough. But he didn't. Eldridge did right by Marceline and me. The least I can do is to repay that kindness and do right by him—that means, in part, keeping his department running smoothly—and it also means not sitting back while the sheriff and his people stumble along, trampling on clues. It means taking an active part in finding him," Zane concluded.

She was moved by his passion and his dedication. "What can I do to help, Mr. Colton?"

He smiled at her offer. The woman really was very sweet, he thought.

"I'll let you know," he promised, although he really doubted there was anything she could do to help him find his father, which was his top priority at this moment and would continue to be until Eldridge was finally found.

They got back to the office building rather quickly. Mirabella returned his car back to its designated parking space, and then they rode up to the twenty-third floor together. Despite the fact that he was understandably preoccupied, Zane still couldn't help noticing the queasy look on Mirabella's face. It seemed to get more pronounced as the elevator bypassed all the lower floors and went straight up to their floor in what felt like record time.

The swift ascent had all but drained the little color from her face, bringing in its stead an exceedingly pained, pale hue.

The moment the elevator door slid open, Mirabella vacated the silver enclosure. In his estimation, she seemed rather unsteady on her feet.

"I'll be back in a moment," she said, making a beeline for the ladies' room.

The woman definitely belonged home. He watched as she disappeared into the bathroom farther down the hall.

He was debating following her and placing himself next to the ladies' room door. If he heard her being sick, he was going to insist she get herself checked out by her own physician. He didn't want to be responsible for her ruining her health.

However, right at that moment, he felt his cell phone vibrating in his jacket pocket.

Now what? he couldn't help wondering, exasperated. Swiping his finger along the bottom of the screen, he braced himself as he said, "Zane Colton."

"Mr. Colton," the voice on the other end of the line said, "it's Meyer."

Zane instantly snapped to attention. "Have you got a name for me, Meyer?"

"Not yet, sir," the man said apologetically. "Unfortunately, there's a great deal of decryption to wade through. It's taking longer than I thought, but I'm getting closer. I did find out the payments stopped a couple of days before your stepfather was kidnapped. That might have been motive enough for someone to kidnap him."

Hopefully it wasn't motive enough for someone to kill him, Zane thought.

Chapter 5

Zane was just putting his cell phone back into his jacket pocket when he saw Mirabella coming out of the restroom. Rather than pale, his administrative assistant's face was now a shade closer to pea green.

Deeply concerned, he momentarily forgot about the call he'd just received. Instead, Zane turned his attention to his assistant's welfare. Crossing to her, he touched her forearm. Her skin felt almost clammy to his fingertips.

Since she'd been ignoring his advice, he raised his voice when he spoke to her. "Belle, I insist you go see a doctor and get checked out. You can't continue like this."

Mirabella offered him a weak smile, unable to do anything more than that. She felt as if all of her strength had been sapped. Although she did feel worse than she had previously, she knew she just had to tough it out. This would fade soon enough, just the way it had been doing for the last couple of months.

"I'm fine, Mr. Colton. Really. It's just a little upset stomach I can't… I can't…seem to…shake."

The last word was uttered in a whisper, if that loud. The hallway had begun to spin and then her surroundings, usually so well lit, began to darken as well as shrink, until everything went completely black around her.

One moment he was speaking with Mirabella, trying in vain to talk some sense into her, the next moment her eyes were rolling back in her head and he saw her literally begin to sink right in front of him. Stunned, Zane barely had time to react.

Moving quickly, he caught Mirabella in his arms and kept her body from crumpling down to the floor.

Panicked, he tried to rouse her. "Belle? Belle, are you all right? No, damn it, of course you're not," he snapped angrily, a helpless feeling sweeping right through him.

"Need help, Mr. Colton?" Nancy, one of the newest employees who'd been hired when the security section had expanded, asked as she ran up.

The fewer people involved, the better, he couldn't help thinking. He knew Mirabella wouldn't appreciate people staring.

"No, I'll handle it," he told the other woman. The next moment, he picked the unconscious assistant up into his arms.

"Are you sure?" Nancy called after him.

"I'm sure. Thanks," he answered without looking back. With that, he carried Mirabella into his office.

He missed the knowing looks exchanged between Nancy and another woman who had just come out to see what the commotion was all about.

Closing the door to his office with his elbow, Zane gently lay the woman down on his sofa.

She was still unconscious.

At a loss as to what to do, he briefly contemplated loosening Mirabella's clothing, but quickly vetoed that idea. She wasn't having any trouble getting air in. Mirabella had apparently fainted for an entirely different reason.

A state-of-the-art bathroom, complete with a sink and shower, was part of his office suite. Zane went to get a wet towel.

Returning quickly, he laid it across Mirabella's forehead, hoping that might help rouse her.

If it didn't work, his next step was to call for an ambulance, something he had a feeling Mirabella wouldn't want.

Adjusting the compress on her forehead, he stepped back and unconsciously held his breath as he watched her intently.

A few seconds later, he saw Mirabella's eyes begin to flutter open.

Thank God.

She began to struggle, trying to get into a sitting position. Zane gently pushed her back down.

"Don't try to get up just yet," he warned.

Disoriented, it took Mirabella a moment to get her bearings and a few more to focus in on her surroundings. The last thing she remembered was being in the hallway, talking to Zane.

"Where am I?" Her brain felt as if it was wrapped in heavy gauze.

"I brought you into my office. You fainted."

As familiarity dawned on her, followed closely by embarrassment, Mirabella tried to bolt upright. "No, I didn't," she protested.

He wasn't about to argue with her. "Have it your way. You took a short nap and would have wound up at my feet if I hadn't caught you."

Her head felt as if it was emerging out of a tailspin. Even so, she couldn't just lie here. That would be totally unprofessional. This was Zane's office.

Clutching the side of the sofa, she swung her legs down until she could feel the floor beneath her feet. Taking a deep breath, she began to rise, only to feel her legs growing wobbly.

She had no choice but to sink down into the sofa again as she struggled to pull herself together.

"Sorry," she murmured.

Zane made no reply. Watching her, it suddenly hit him what was going on. Putting his hand on her shoulder to press her down again as she tried for a second time to gain her footing, he sat down next to her.

He shook his head. How could he have not seen this before?

"You know," he told her, "I can be pretty dense sometimes."

"I'm not sure what you mean," she heard herself saying.

Her voice sounded distant and tinny to her ear. Mirabella was still having a great deal of difficulty focusing on the room. She clenched her hands in her lap, unaware she was clutching the towel he'd placed on her forehead. Her mind scrambled for a way to explain herself out of this. She didn't want him or anyone else knowing the truth, at least not yet.

"What I mean," he replied patiently, "is I don't always pick up on all the clues that are right there in front of me."

Her breath caught in her throat as her heart seemed to stand still for a moment.

Had Zane guessed the crush she had harbored for him all this time had turned into something that was now a great deal more? Did he know his every kindness had warmed her heart and that she had begun to see him as something other than just her boss? Did he suspect that lately he'd begun to enter her dreams on almost a nightly basis?

Mirabella racked her brain, trying to come up with something to deflect his suspicions, if it wasn't already too late.

But before she could come up with any sort of a reply, Zane rendered her entirely speechless by asking, "You're pregnant, aren't you?"

Her mouth dropped open and she could only stare at him in total silence. Her mind went blank and words completely failed her.

"I take that as a yes," he commented in response to her total silence.

What he didn't comment on, either to her or to himself, was how the realization of Mirabella's apparent delicate condition suddenly created wide, stinging holes through his entire being.

He found himself feeling vastly disappointed and

he couldn't even begin to explain, to himself and certainly not to her, why. After all, he wasn't one of those supermoralists who professed to know what was best not just for himself but for everyone else around him.

As far as he was concerned, he'd always espoused a philosophy of live and let live. What that meant was he believed everyone had a perfect right to live their lives the way they wanted to, as long as no one else was hurt in the process.

But that was just it, he realized. This *did* hurt. It hurt a great deal.

Finding out Mirabella was pregnant, that there was a man in her life, someone she'd cared enough about to sleep with—because he *knew* she wasn't the type to have careless, meaningless sex with just anyone—somehow felt as if it crushed his very soul.

Damn it, Colton, get over it. She's your administrative assistant, not your long lost soul mate, a small voice in his head insisted.

Usually, that small voice had a great deal of wisdom going for it. But this time around, Zane just wasn't so sure.

Still feeling shaky, Mirabella told herself that she couldn't just continue sitting there, saying nothing while Zane made assumptions. Dead-on assumptions, unfortunately, but still, she had to say something to defend herself. To not say anything made her seem either stupid, or indifferent to her situation.

Or just plain brazen.

She was none of those. She never had been. What she was, Mirabella thought, was completely overwhelmed. Never in her wildest dreams did she believe she would *ever* be in this sort of a situation. She'd thought if she ever did find herself pregnant, it would be because it had been a conscious choice on her part.

Hers and her husband's.

Instead, things had just happened around her without her actual consent. This was *not* how she'd envisioned her life.

Mirabella clenched her hands into fists on either side of her. She absolutely *refused* to allow herself to behave like a victim. And in order to *not* be a victim, she had to get out in front of this situation, had to take charge of it as well as of the rest of her life. Her pride would allow for nothing less.

"Yes," she replied in a quiet voice.

"Yes?" he repeated, uncertain exactly what she was saying yes to.

The time lapse between when he'd stopped talking and she had just spoken up had been large enough to leave a great deal of room for confusion. And right now he was confused as well as disappointed.

"Yes, you're right," she told him stoically. "I am pregnant."

Again, he felt as if he'd just been sucker punched. Upbraiding himself that there was no reason for him to feel this way didn't seem to change anything.

"Are congratulations in order?" he asked in a subdued voice.

He assumed, since Mirabella was making this admission, she intended to keep the baby, but he wasn't about to take anything for granted, just in case. He waited to be told her intentions.

"Right now," she replied honestly, "I'm not sure just what's in order. I'll let you know when—and *if*—I ever stop being so damn sick."

Zane remained sitting on the sofa, shifting slightly so he was now on the far edge. He didn't want to appear to be crowding her.

"Have you been to see a doctor?" he asked her. Her welfare was still his main concern.

"Oh, yes," she told him with exaggerated feeling. It was the doctor who had indifferently informed her of her condition.

Zane picked up on her tone of voice. "The doctor wasn't reassuring?"

"If by that you mean did he tell me about my options, yes, he did. To quote him, I could either 'have it, or not have it.' And," she continued, trying not to allow her emotions to break through, "if I went with door number one, I still didn't have to keep it once the 'residency' period was up. I could always give it up for adoption," she said, quoting the doctor.

The conversation she'd had with the doctor had left her so cold and numb, she'd spent the rest of the day and part of the next crying.

"What are you going to do?" Zane asked her, forgetting for the moment that as her boss, he had no right to ask her questions of such a personal, probing nature.

She took a deep breath, squaring her shoulders. "I'll let you know the second I stop throwing up everything but the kitchen sink so I can think clearly."

Mirabella felt another wave coming over her and fought to keep it from overwhelming her. She pressed her hand against her stomach as if that could somehow contain and subdue the pending waves of nausea and keep them from coming up.

"If this is what it feels like, why would any woman

in her right mind ever want to be pregnant?" she asked miserably.

He was doing his best to maintain a professional distance, but he just couldn't help feeling sympathetic about what she was going through.

"I'm definitely no expert, but I don't think it feels like that for every woman," he told her. "And from what I've heard, a lot of women think it's all really worth it—once they get to hold their baby in their arms."

Zane paused for a moment, debating whether or not to ask her the next question. It turned out to be a very short debate.

"How does the baby's father feel about all this?"

Mirabella stiffened, inadvertently recalling the man's parting words to her. Words she had no desire to repeat. Nor did she want to remember anything about him, because he had turned out to be so very different from the man he had pretended to be.

But that was on her, Mirabella thought the next moment. How naive could she have been not to realize some men would say anything just to get what they were after? It wasn't as if she'd lived a sheltered life, she knew these things happened, that there were men—a *lot* of men—who lied.

The problem was, she didn't realize this could happen to her, that someone would knowingly and deliberately lie to *her*. The very fact that this had happened to her made her feel violated.

But she was determined it wouldn't destroy her.

She turned her head to look at Zane. "I'd rather not talk about that if you don't mind," she replied a little formally.

It was his cue to pull back, to drop the subject that wasn't any of his business to begin with.

But because Mirabella was his administrative assistant, because he interacted with her every day and relied on her being as efficient as she had been up until now, for this as well so many other reasons, her well-being was his concern.

In his view, the term *well-being* encompassed a great deal of territory.

"But he does know, right?" he prodded, watching Mirabella's face for a telltale clue. "The baby's father does know about its existence? You did tell him, right?" He wanted to know.

Mirabella shifted uncomfortably. It felt decidedly strange to her to be thinking about Kyle in the present tense now that he was dead. But the fact that he was dead really didn't change anything. She didn't want to admit to having slept with him, which, in turn, was to admit to being used by him.

In her eyes it made her seem like a little fool—and worse. But since Zane was obviously not letting go of this, she made the nebulous admission and hoped that would be enough for him.

"Yes, I told him. Now, if you don't mind, I'd like to drop the subject." She began to get up. "I'd—"

She stopped abruptly as another wave of nausea, this one far more intense than its immediate predecessor, suddenly caught her up in its grip. She dug the fingernails of her left hand into the arm of the sofa as if that could somehow channel the sensation she was feeling out of her body and into the inanimate object.

It couldn't.

Caught up in all this, Zane saw that horrid color—

pea green—reemerge and all but paint her complexion from the throat up.

He could see by the sudden panicked look in her eyes that she felt she wasn't going to be able to make it down the hall in time.

He wasn't about to allow her to embarrass herself in front of the other people on the floor. They were, in general, good people. But a lot of good people still loved to gossip. Some actually thrived on it, he recalled.

With that in mind, Zane quickly got to his feet and out of her way.

"Use my bathroom," he volunteered. He saw she was about to demur and he quickly cut her off. "You're not going to make it down the hall. Now stop being so damn stubborn about everything and use the blasted bathroom," he ordered, pushing open the door to the pristine restroom.

She wanted to protest and tell him that she was going to use the ladies' room since it was available to everyone. But she never got the chance.

Her words were blocked by the sensation of something ominous about to reappear at any second and it was going to be right here, on his rug, if she didn't hustle and take advantage of the generous offer he'd just made to her.

She felt there was a time for pride and a time for practicality and this definitely fell into the latter category.

Wanting to murmur "thank you" but afraid if she so much as opened her mouth, they would both deeply regret it, she could only nod at him as she dashed past Zane and straight into the bathroom.

Knowing she would welcome privacy as much as he would welcome not having to hear anything he'd prefer not to, Zane pulled the door closed behind her.

Just in time.

The next moment, he heard a knock on his outer door.

Chapter 6

Zane's first thought was he needed to get rid of whoever was on the other side of his office door before Mirabella emerged from his bathroom. That seemingly innocent event could very easily start rumors and rumors of *any* sort were the last thing he needed to deal with right now. He'd learned from personal experience that people were capable of taking a tidbit of what they perceived to be information and somehow wound up spinning the complete works of William Shakespeare out of it.

Crossing quickly toward the door, Zane pulled it open.

Any thought of sending the person off instantly vanished when he saw who it was.

In his midthirties and balding, Meyer Stanley had a slight build. He obsessively maintained ramrod straight posture in an effort to appear at least a little taller than his five-foot-five-inch stature. He succeeded only in making himself look like a determined swizzle stick when he walked.

His most outstanding feature, despite the black framed glasses he wore—or perhaps because of them—was his eyes. As he walked into Zane's office, Meyer's eyes appeared so huge, they were almost startling.

To say Zane was surprised to see the IT expert was putting it mildly.

"I just talked to you a few minutes ago," Zane said. Had Meyer forgotten to add something?

Meyer bobbed his head up and down. His glasses slid down his nose, and he pushed them back up with a jerky motion of his index finger.

"Yes, I know." The three words came out sounding almost breathless.

Zane took a guess as to why the man had felt compelled to suddenly rush over. "Did you find out where my father's money was being wired?"

Again Meyer nodded vigorously in response. When he spoke, his voice had dropped several octaves from its usual high-pitched tone. But before he spoke, he looked furtively around, as if he wanted to make sure there was no one else in the room who would overhear what he was about to say.

"I thought it was best if I came to tell you this in person."

Zane had worked with Meyer for a couple of years now, albeit in a different division, and knew the man had a flair for the dramatic. But this was a level he'd never witnessed before. Zane had absolutely no idea what to expect.

An uneasiness began to work its way through his system, although he continued to maintain a perfect poker face.

"Go ahead."

"The regular transfers from one of your father's bank accounts—when they were being made," Meyer qualified, trying to be painstakingly accurate, "were going into an encrypted bank account belonging to—"

Meyer paused, not for any sort of dramatic effect, but because he was obviously nervous about the disclosure he was about to make.

Zane couldn't remember ever seeing the IT expert behave this way. Just how damning was this discovery Meyer had made?

"Go ahead, out with it, Meyer," Zane ordered. "Who did the account belong to?"

Meyer swallowed. "It belonged to—"

A noise from the side of the office caught his attention. Meyer looked around Zane's arm and he saw the bathroom door being opened. Someone was coming out.

When Meyer saw who it was, he appeared stunned as his mouth dropped open and he seemed to actually shake a little, as well.

"Damn it, Meyer, who?" Zane demanded, calling the man's attention back to him. "C'mon, man. Spit it out. Give me a name. Who did the encrypted account turn out to belong to?"

Behaving like a man who had suddenly lost the ability to form words, Meyer was temporarily reduced to having to point. Which he did.

Straight at Mirabella.

"Her," he finally croaked out nervously. "The account belongs to your administrative assistant. Mirabella Freeman." The damning words came out in breathless gulps. The next moment, Meyer was thrusting a folded up sheet of paper at him.

Taking it, Zane opened the paper and quickly scanned it. His expression hardened. Everything was right there, condemning her as the one on the receiving end of Eldridge Colton's regular bank withdrawals.

Hearing her name, Mirabella stopped dead in her tracks. She looked from Zane to the funny little man he liked to use whenever he was confronted with cyber puzzles or things of a similar, challenging nature.

Something was going on and from the way the two men had looked at her, Mirabella had a feeling it wasn't good.

"Did I miss something?" she asked, deciding it best to meet whatever this was head-on. How bad could it be? She hadn't been in the bathroom *that* long, Mirabella reasoned, although when she was throwing up, every second felt like an eternity to her—an awful eternity.

Zane didn't answer her.

The silence grew more ominous.

He didn't say anything about what was going on or why Meyer was in his office. In the flash of an instant, given one piece of information he'd gotten from Meyer, everything had changed.

He focused his attention entirely on Meyer, trying to keep the information the man had just given him at bay for as long as he could.

His eyes narrowed as he looked at Meyer. "You're sure about that?"

The man's face was the epitome of solemnity. "That's where the trail ended, sir," Meyer replied.

Ordinarily, Mirabella knew when to refrain from saying anything. She might be Zane's administrative assistant, but it wasn't her place to interfere in his conversations. If he wanted to bring her into it, he would have indicated as much.

But she had this uneasy feeling whatever was going on was somehow about her and she couldn't very well defend herself if she didn't know what she was defending herself against or from.

She needed answers.

"What is this all about?" Mirabella asked.

The question was directed to Zane, but when he didn't answer her, her eyes shifted to Meyer. She thought she detected a glimpse of pity in the IT's brown eyes before he lowered them, appearing as if he was trying to find a lost penny in the rug's thick beige pile.

"That'll be all, Meyer," Zane said, dismissing the tech. "Let me know if those transfers happen to start up again."

"Absolutely," Meyer promised, apparently relieved to be leaving the office. He slipped out the door as unobtrusively as a business envelope slipped through a mail slot.

"When *what* transfers start up again?" Mirabella asked.

Zane was deliberately keeping her in the dark and the longer that went on, the more uneasy she became. Did he think she was involved in Eldridge's kidnapping? Had he asked his trusty information ferret to uncover the identity of her baby's father because he believed that was somehow tied to the kidnapping?

You're overthinking this and giving yourself too much credit. Zane doesn't care who you slept with, as long as it doesn't wind up reflecting badly on, or embarrassing, the company. Grow up! she ordered herself.

There was no actual reason for her to believe Zane was taking an interest in her—certainly not a personal one.

But when he turned around to face her, his expression frozen in a dark look she couldn't begin to fathom, Mirabella wasn't sure what to think—only that whatever information Zane had just gotten from Meyer had apparently made him very angry.

The next moment, the need to guess was terminated.

"Why was my father depositing almost ten thousand dollars every month into your encrypted bank account?" he wanted to know, his voice harsh and unyielding.

She stared at Zane, the man she regarded as her boss and so much more. The words he had just uttered bounced off her head as if they'd been voiced in some language that was completely foreign to her.

"Into my *what*?" she cried, unable to process what he was asking.

His face darkened. He was in no mood to play games with someone he felt had betrayed him in too many ways to count.

"You heard me," he retorted. Then, because she continued looking at him uncomprehendingly, he repeated the last part of his question. "Into your *en-crypted* bank account."

The room had begun to spin around her again and her knees had gone completely weak. Her hand out, searching for something to brace herself against, Mirabella stumbled back to the sofa.

The next second, she collapsed into it.

Zane almost reached out to steady her, but then he pulled back his hand. She was playing him again, he thought angrily.

Well, not this time, honey.

"Please, spare me the act," Zane told her coldly. "That worked once, but I'm not being taken in a second time."

She made no effort to protest it was an act. She was barely holding on to consciousness by the edge of her fingertips. She could feel perspiration forming a damp ring just beneath her hairline.

Mirabella dragged in a ragged breath, desperately trying to make sense out of what her boss was telling her.

"What are you talking about?" she demanded with as much angry indignation as she could summon. She still failed to sound forceful, only extremely shaken. "I don't *have* an encrypted bank account and the only account I *do* have certainly doesn't have nearly twenty thousand dollars in it—"

"Almost thirty thousand," Zane corrected, his eyes never leaving her face.

He was going to get the truth out of her if it killed him, Zane silently vowed.

Her eyes appeared to be both stunned and blazing as she raised them to his.

"It doesn't have that amount in it, either," she insisted. "What you're saying is crazy. Why would Mr. Eldridge put that much money into an account with my name on it?" She wanted to know.

Mr. Eldridge. As if you hadn't been warming my father's sheets, preying on his weakening state of health and mind, Zane thought in disgust.

He'd trusted her. How could she have done that? How *could* she?

He said, "That's what I'm trying to find out."

She'd had about enough. And since he'd already condemned her, she really didn't have anything to lose anymore.

"Well, let me make it easy for you," Mirabella retorted. "He wouldn't. I don't know where you got this insane idea from, but it's just not true," she declared heatedly.

Meyer, working his wizardry, had uncovered the bank account's actual number as well as its location and the name of the account owner. The IT had handed that over to him before leaving just now.

"I got the initial 'idea' from the sheriff," Zane informed her. "He was the one who discovered the regular withdrawals from my father's account into some untraceable account. I gave that information to Meyer who followed up on it and tracked down the name of the culprit behind the scheme." His eyes narrowed. "That answer your question for you?"

His tone was so cold, she felt she needed a winter coat to withstand being in its presence without getting frostbite.

But rather than cower or just accept his censure,

Mirabella stood her ground and said defiantly, "All except for why."

Her words didn't make any sense. "Why what?" Zane bit off angrily.

She was easygoing up to a point, but that point had just been passed.

She raised her chin, every inch a fighter who was not about to accept defeat quietly. "Why would someone want to frame me?"

He stared at Mirabella for a long moment, realizing he would have wanted nothing more than to believe her. But evidence was evidence and he trusted Meyer implicitly. The man didn't know *how* to lie.

"Someone framed you," Zane echoed with barely harnessed contempt. "Is that the excuse you're going with?"

"Yes," she retorted angrily, afraid that at any second, she was going to burst into tears. "That's what I'm going with. Because it's the truth," she insisted.

Damn, I wish I could believe you. "Well, here's the way I see it," Zane said. "You and my father had an affair. Maybe you even tricked him into it, I don't know," he said, speaking fast in order to talk over the protest he saw she was about to voice. "But you did and you deliberately didn't take any precautions, hoping to get pregnant so you could blackmail my father and get him to pay you any amount of money you asked for in exchange for your silence."

He glared at her, blocking feelings of betrayal he had absolutely no idea how to handle. "Am I getting warmer?" Zane asked sarcastically.

"I don't know, just how hot is hell?" she retorted furiously. "Because that's where you're obviously going to go for even *thinking* something like that about me or about that sweet old man." Fully fired up, she told Zane exactly what she was thinking—she saw no reason to hold back any longer. "I respect your father, I like your father—maybe I even *love* your father—but I love him *like* a father, not like someone I would ever, *ever*—"

Exasperated, Mirabella couldn't even get herself to finish her sentence. Instead, she made a small, guttural sound reflecting her total frustration about the entire preposterous idea he had just outlined.

How could he even entertain such an idea about her? Was that how little regard he had for her?

She blew out a shaky breath and then attempted to draw in a more steadying one in order to continue giving him a piece of her mind.

But at least for now, her own indignation prevented her from saying anything that sounded even the least bit remotely coherent.

Mirabella took another breath, and then, as calmly as she was able, measuring out each word, she told Zane, "If that's what you really believe about me, then, regretfully, I have to hand in my resignation. I can't work for anyone who actually regards me—regards my *character*—in such awful terms."

She rose to her feet too quickly and suffered the consequences.

The room began to spin again and for one mortifying moment, Mirabella thought she was going to pass out for the second time that day.

Grabbing hold of the sofa's arm, she continued holding on to it until the room finally slowed down and ceased moving.

Zane, on the outside chance she actually *was* going

to faint, quickly moved to her side. He reached for her to take hold of her shoulders.

Mirabella angrily pushed one of his hands aside with the flat of her own.

"I can manage," she informed him through gritted teeth. "You wouldn't want to be seen grabbing your father's *kept woman*," Mirabella warned in a mocking voice. "Heaven only knows what kind of stories *that* would give birth to."

He supposed maybe this could all be just an elaborate performance. After all, if Mirabella had done what he'd just accused her of, she could very well feign this indignation in order to play the part of a wronged woman in his eyes.

He just didn't know anymore.

So much had happened in this last month that he found himself at a loss as to what to believe and what to hold suspect. Truth had become a very elusive commodity, changing its appearance to the point that he didn't know if he could actually recognize it anymore. Truth had become a chameleon, assuming odd shapes.

And then he thought he heard the little voice in his head advise, *Trust your gut*.

He hadn't worked his way up in the company—and in Eldridge's estimation, by looking to others for guidance, or by relying on reports and other people's opinions to dictate his actions. He'd done it by following his own instincts.

In a nutshell, by trusting his gut.

And his gut told him the woman he had relied on all this time, who had worked tirelessly at his side without expectation of praise or any sort of additional compensation these last few years, was telling him the truth.

That she was being framed.

Just before Mirabella reached the door, fully intending to slam it on her exit as a final statement of both protest and anger, she heard Zane ask, "Then it's not my father's baby?"

Part of her just wanted to keep going, refusing to even dignify Zane's question with any sort of a response. But there was something in his tone that made her turn around.

And once she did, she had to answer him.

"No," she said firmly, placing one protective hand over the nonexistent bump in her stomach, "this is most definitely *not* your father's baby."

Chapter 7

Doing her best to cover up the hurt she felt, that Zane would even *think* something like this about her, that he didn't seem to be able to recall all the times they'd worked together, all the times she'd gone above the call of duty to provide the backup he'd needed, Mirabella delivered what she hoped would be the final death knell to the ridiculous theory he'd sprung on her.

"And to put what you'd just so ludicrously accused me of to rest once and for all," she informed him crisply, "once the baby is born, I'll even agree to a paternity test."

Zane didn't reply at first. He remained silent for what seemed like a very long time.

The awkward moment stretched out, growing more uncomfortable by the second. And then, finally, he said, "I believe you."

The hurt inside her refused to abate. Zane's lack of faith, however temporary, had done a great deal of damage to her emotional state at what felt like almost lightning speed.

Mirabella looked at him now, not experiencing any sense of even minor relief or camaraderie. Zane had demolished all that and it was going to take time— perhaps a great deal of time—before it could be rebuilt. Right now, the way she felt, she wasn't even sure it ever could be.

"I really don't care if you do or not," Mirabella told him. "I just don't want to be caught up in the fallout from a lie."

Zane nodded, but even as he did so, he felt compelled to ask her, "Who is the father?" even though he was fully aware he was still stepping well out of the boundaries of a boss-employee relationship.

Mirabella looked at him, stunned.

"That is none of your business," she replied coldly. "But I will tell you—even though I don't have to—it is *not* your father and it's not anyone you need to worry about," Mirabella concluded.

Since the father of her unborn child was dead, his name would make no difference to Zane one way or another. His identity was her secret to reveal or keep and she chose to keep it.

Zane and Mirabella had a good working relationship up until just now and he felt badly about what felt like its apparent demise. He'd been upset and stressed to almost the breaking point, but that wasn't an excuse to suddenly turn on her and believe the worst. She'd never given him any cause for that.

He'd just gotten caught up in this storm and had

lost the ability to know who—or what—to believe. He shouldn't have.

"Mirabella." He began feeling his way to an apology, something he had very little experience with. "I'm sorry if I offended you—"

"If?" Mirabella echoed incredulously, her eyes wide with disbelief. *"If?"*

He really *wasn't* any good at this. Zane tried again. "You're right. I'm sorry I offended you. But I've been under a great deal of stress lately," he explained, hoping that would be enough to make her understand his rather abrupt, erratic behavior.

She appreciated the fact that he was trying to make amends, but it was going to take a lot more than that for her to forgive him and come around.

"Did it ever occur to you that you're not the only one in that sort of a situation?" she asked.

Zane blew out a breath. She was right, of course. He'd been so angry, he had never even considered she might have been wrongly accused. He'd just jumped at the logical conclusion—or what he'd believed was the logical conclusion at the time—given the information he had to work with.

From the look on her face, he wasn't sure she would ever forgive him. And in all honesty, he couldn't really blame her.

All he could do was restate the obvious—and hope for the best. "Again, I'm sorry," Zane apologized.

Rather than tell him that she accepted his apology, Mirabella merely nodded in response.

It wasn't in her heart to harbor a grudge.

"All right, I'll take it under advisement," she replied, echoing a phrase he had used on several occasions.

The clipped, detached phrase made him smile. "That's all I can ask."

Joining her at his door, Zane opened it for her, then stepped to the side, the perfect gentleman.

The moment she walked out of the room, Zane was back on the phone, calling Meyer. The assignment was far from complete.

Meyer Stanley picked up his phone on the third ring.

"Stanley," the IT expert declared.

"I want you to find out who set up that encrypted account at the bank."

It took the man on the other end a moment to realize who was calling him. But even so, he still didn't understand why. Zane's request sounded almost redundant to him.

"I thought we already have the answer to that," Meyer protested.

"No," Zane corrected evenly, then went on to explain the difference. "We know whose account the money was coming out of and supposedly whose it was going into. We made certain assumptions about what was going on, but we didn't bother verifying those assumptions," he pointed out.

He could all but see Meyer squirming in his chair. The oversight was obviously on him.

"It just seemed self-evident," Meyer argued weakly.

He couldn't very well blame Meyer when he was guilty of the same oversight. Zane went easy on the tech expert. "That's undoubtedly what the person who set this all in motion thought."

"Mr. Colton," Meyer began in a shaky voice, "I'm so sorry—"

"Don't be sorry, Meyer, be thorough," Zane instructed. "*Sorry* doesn't do either one of us any good," he told him, thinking of his own apology to Mirabella. "And just for the record, we both made the same obvious mistake," he said. "Now find out, beyond a shadow of a doubt," he stipulated, "who authorized those transfers.

"And while you're at it," he added, "find out if any money was withdrawn from that encrypted account once it was deposited. If it was—" and he really hoped it was "—I want to know by whom."

"Yes, sir," Meyer was quick to agree. And then he said rather sheepishly, "I guess this isn't really over yet."

Zane laughed shortly. Someone had intentionally misled him and he wanted to know why. "Not by a long shot. And Meyer—"

"Yes, sir?" the man asked, sounding instantly on the alert.

"I don't think I need to tell you all this is to be kept strictly confidential." There was a warning note in his voice—just in case.

"No, sir. I mean, yes, sir. I mean—" Tongue-tied, the IT expert was at a complete loss just how to make himself understood.

Taking pity on the man, Zane let him off the hook. "That's okay, Meyer. Just get me those results," he ordered.

"Yes, sir, right away, sir."

Zane could almost visualize the man bowing and

backing out of the room, the way servants had done in the presence of a king. He shook his head.

"Goodbye, Meyer."

Terminating the call, Zane replaced the receiver into its cradle and then rocked back in his chair as he stared unseeingly at the multilined telephone. He'd thought his life was complicated before any of this had started. Now the situation was way beyond anything he could even begin to adequately describe.

A little more than a month ago, all he'd had to deal with were packed schedules and overlapping appointments. And the biggest things he'd had to contend with were disgruntled employees and bored hackers who saw breaking into his company's system—his company's *secured* system—as a challenge and a way to keep their boredom at bay for a few days or, most likely, a few hours.

Now he was faced with a possible life-or-death situation to resolve.

Life or death.

Life, not death.

He had to believe his father was among the former and not the latter, otherwise, he didn't think he would really be able to proceed. His grief would get the better of him—not to mention Watkins would probably be hauling him down to the sheriff's office again for another round of intense questioning regarding his father's murder.

Zane knew he couldn't be Watkins's only suspect in his father's kidnapping, but right now, it certainly felt as though he was.

Zane sighed, glancing out his window at the cloudless sky. He *really* wanted to go out, to get some air, stretch his legs and his mind, but he knew for the time being, it would be for the best if he just remained where he was and played the part of the good little head of security.

With effort, Zane forced himself to process some of the paperwork he'd been putting off.

The work wasn't going to do itself no matter how much chaos there was around him.

Preoccupied, Zane nearly jumped at the unexpected sound. His landline was ringing. Although his immediate instinct was to pick up the receiver, he looked at caller ID before doing so.

Meyer.

It had been almost a full day since he'd given Meyer his instructions about tracking down the name of the person who had authorized the monthly transfers out of his father's account and into the account with Mirabella's name on it. This was the first time the man was getting back to him.

Since finding the information was a top priority, and because it was taking this much time, obviously whoever they were dealing with was good at what he or she did. The perpetrator knew the ins and outs of banking as well as how to successfully manipulate the internet to do his or her bidding. What the person was doing, Zane thought darkly, was in essence taking a good thing and making it do something bad.

There always seemed to be a real downside to progress, Zane thought as he brought the receiver to his ear.

"Got anything for me, Meyer?" he asked without waiting for the tech expert to say anything first.

"You were right, boss," Meyer declared. "It's your

father's account, but he didn't authorize any withdrawals to be made, regularly or otherwise."

At this point, Meyer wasn't telling him anything he hadn't already suspected, Zane thought impatiently.

"Who did?" He wanted to know.

"I can't say yet," Meyer admitted, sounding embarrassed. "All I know is whoever did it knew what they were doing. But I'm not giving up, sir," he quickly added with feeling.

"I don't pay you to give up," Zane reminded him before hanging up.

Zane was aware that sounded harsh, but right now he wasn't in a very forgiving, jovial mood. Someone out there was deliberately playing mind games and trying to throw him off the scent. Exactly to what end he had no idea yet.

He supposed it could be just random maliciousness—or it could be perceived as payback of some sort, with the intent of eventually bringing down the entire Colton corporation.

Until he had some sort of definitive answers, he had no idea what it was that he was fighting. It put him at a very bad disadvantage, like a prizefighter boxing with one hand tied behind his back.

A movement on his monitor caught his attention and he turned his chair around to look at it. Just before the call from Meyer had come in, he'd been studying a spreadsheet on his screen, but it seemed to have disappeared.

In its stead was what appeared to be a company-wide email.

Colton Incorporated's logo was at the top, and while the email was addressed to "all Colton Incorporated employees," the sender did not bear the name of any of the department heads.

Instead, the email appeared to have been sent by the ever popular—and inaccessible—"Anonymous." It went from bad to worse. The email's subject line declared: Zane Colton is the Father of Mirabella Freeman's Unborn Child.

Zane felt an icy cold chill run down his spine as he read the words that followed.

Mirabella Freeman, Zane Colton's administrative assistant, gives new meaning to the term "fringe benefits." Apparently, when she found herself (or deliberately got herself) pregnant with Zane Colton's baby, Ms. Freeman gave as good as she got. Some of you might be interested to know—I certainly was—that company money supposedly in Eldridge Colton's name—our apparently "kidnapped" founder—is being wired into an account which was just recently discovered to belong to the pregnant Ms. Freeman. This is obviously payoff money from Zane Colton—who's not even a real Colton! This sort of thing shouldn't be condoned while good people are slaving away for a company that's being run by decadent narcissists who are only out for themselves.

Stunned, Zane read the email again.

And then a third time.

He kept hoping his eyes were transposing words or even seeing words that weren't actually there.

But his eyes weren't playing tricks on him. All three readings yielded the same sick feeling in the pit of his stomach.

It took everything he had to suppress the rage he felt bubbling up inside of him.

And then he thought he heard a cry of pain mixed with what sounded like sheer anguish and distress. It was coming from just outside his office.

Mirabella.

Something had gone very wrong.

He was instantly on his feet. Throwing open the door, Zane looked out. "Belle, are you all right?"

She turned in her chair to face him and he saw her stricken face. "No," she answered in an almost eerily still voice, "I'm not all right." And then her voice grew in volume as she asked, horrified, "Who wrote this awful email?"

Glancing at her screen just to be sure, he saw she had received the same email. "I don't know," he told her, "but if I find them, they better hope their insurance is all paid up." It was as far as Zane would allow his anger to go in front of her. She was already visibly shaken and upset. He didn't want to add to it by ranting or venting his anger. "Get Meyer Stanley on the phone," he ordered.

Before Mirabella could pick up the receiver and comply, her phone began to ring insistently.

As did his.

It was as if their phones had suddenly triggered a cacophony of other ringing phones.

Mirabella's hand seemed to visibly shake as he watched her pick up her landline's receiver.

"Mr. Colton's office," she said almost inaudibly, as if afraid of what she was about to hear.

She wasn't wrong.

"Congratulations. You found the secret to sleeping your way to the top, slut," a voice on the other end snarled.

Mirabella didn't bother answering the accusation or defending herself. Instead, she slammed the receiver into its cradle. When it bounced back out again, moved by the force of the slam, Zane returned it to its cradle for her.

Her hard breathing answered any lingering questions Zane might have had regarding the nature of the phone call she'd just received.

"Don't let it get to you," he advised gently.

Mirabella lifted her chin in almost defiance. "Easy for you to say. You're a Colton. You're not trying to 'sleep your way to the top,'" she retorted as she repeated the caller's taunt, tears filling her eyes despite her anger.

Zane looked past her shoulder at her computer monitor. Emails were coming in at a fast, furious pace. The first one only had one word to it, written in capital letters, employing a sixteen point font so the message wouldn't be overlooked.

As Mirabella began to turn back to her desk, he caught her hand and physically stopped her. Drawing her to her feet, Zane suggested with feeling, "Why don't we get out of here?"

She could *hear* the emails coming in. There was no escaping them or the sentiments they expressed. "And go where?"

"A restaurant, a coffee shop. Anywhere but here," he countered. "It's almost dinnertime," he said the next moment, realizing the hour. "Let's go out and have dinner," he suggested, looking at her. Still holding her hand as if to coax her into agreeing, he added as a final enticement, "It'll be on me."

She began to glance over her shoulder, but again, he stopped her, directing her line of vision forward and toward him.

Mirabella offered him a weak smile. The malicious emails were twisting her stomach, making her feel even sicker than she already was.

She placed her hand on her abdomen, futilely trying to soothe it. "That might be truer than you think," she warned.

He lifted a shoulder in a vague shrug. "That's fine. I'm washable," he told her with a wink. "Now get your purse. I'm taking you home after this."

There was no arguing with his tone. Not that she even wanted to.

Mirabella could literally hear the number of emails multiplying on her screen with every second that passed. Did everyone hate her?

She didn't want to know.

"I need to shut it down," she told Zane, trying to turn toward the computer keyboard.

Zane raised an index finger as if to warn her to remain where she was. The next second, locating it, he pulled the plug out of the wall.

Her monitor went blank.

"It's shut," he declared, gesturing toward the dormant black screen. "Let's go."

Chapter 8

Dumbfounded, Mirabella stared at the black screen before her eyes shifted to Zane. "You can't do that," she cried.

His expression was unfathomable. "I just did," he stated flatly.

She knew this, she had eyes. But that wasn't what she meant.

"But if you don't shut it down properly, you can lose data doing it like that," Mirabella protested. It was a totally reckless, spontaneous action. She hadn't thought he was capable of that.

Zane appeared unfazed by her complaint. "We've got one of the best IT departments in the country. If any data happened to get lost just now, they can restore it. And if, for some reason, they can't, Meyer Stanley can. Meyer could probably find and restore the lost city of Atlantis if he set his mind to it. So stop worrying about company matters and worry about yourself for a change," he admonished. And then he offered what appeared to be a hint of a smile. "Now let's go," Zane urged.

Mirabella still felt uncertain about the fate of the data on her computer. It represented a great deal of work that had been done on her part. But she wasn't very well in a position to argue with Zane, so she nodded her head, giving in.

"You're right," she murmured.

His hand on the doorknob, Zane paused to look at the younger woman.

"Of course I'm right. I'm the boss," he told her, watching her expression carefully as he tried to get her to smile a little.

Though he gave no outward indication of it, inside, he was seething. Not at Mirabella, but at the complete waste of human flesh who was behind this unfounded, malicious gossip. There wasn't so much as an iota of truth to it.

Nor was there anything to base it on. Until his impromptu suggestion about having dinner together, they had never gone out socially together, or so much as attended a party where they were both separately invited.

Yes, there were times—a lot of times, actually— that they'd worked long hours together, but that was exactly all it had been: work. There'd been no secret, stolen moments together, no moments together of *any* kind that didn't include deadlines or security matters.

He'd be lying if he said he didn't find Mirabella attractive. He did. More than just passably so. With hair the color of subdued flame, light brown eyes and a porcelain complexion, Mirabella Freeman was a very beautiful woman.

But he wasn't the type to mix business and pleasure for precisely the reason that had reared its ugly head just now. Zane wanted to take no chances on being compromised. That meant keeping his reputation beyond reproach so his father would always feel he could trust him.

And just where had all of that sterling behavior gotten him? Zane silently mocked himself now. He was being publicly accused of fathering a child he hadn't even known about a couple of days ago. Not just fathering it, but actually *stealing* funds out of his father's bank account in order to pay the baby's mother—his own administrative assistant—hush money.

It didn't get any crazier than that, he thought, looking at Mirabella.

The whole gaggle of lies were so reprehensible, he didn't know where to start to dismantle them.

But what he did know was issuing a rebuttal to the spiteful email and branding it for the lie it was would only make people more convinced than ever it wasn't a lie and they would go right on maliciously believing it.

And while he found all of that irritating and difficult to put up with, he knew he wasn't suffering nearly as much as Mirabella was. It was going to take a long time for him to scrub the image of her face from his mind.

She had looked absolutely stricken when he'd walked into the room. No one should be put through what she was enduring.

He held his office door opened for her. Mirabella

passed over the threshold into the hallway without a word. But she could only keep quiet for so long.

"Isn't this like running away?" Mirabella asked him as they arrived at the bank of elevators and he pressed the down button.

"No," he replied patiently, "this is giving everyone who just read that ridiculous email post a chance to cool off and come to their senses. Because once they do, they'll realize whoever wrote that was just hurling mindless insults around. Vicious insults that are completely baseless," he added vehemently.

He was being too optimistic in his viewpoint, she thought. People loved taking other people down because, for some reason, that somehow raised them up higher. Or so the theory went.

"But…" Mirabella began to protest.

Zane cut her short. "I thought you weren't going to argue with me," he reminded her. "After all, I am the boss."

One of the people in charge of a different division within his security department was walking by just then. The woman, Gloria Winters, had obviously overheard the latter part of his exchange with his administrative assistant and was shaking her head as she frowned in response to what he'd said.

Zane caught the look on the woman's face out of the corner of his eye. "Something wrong, Gloria?" he asked pointedly.

Gloria Winters hadn't realized she'd been so blatant in her censure of her boss and the woman she assumed he was consorting with. Caught and embarrassed, Gloria vigorously shook her head, her voice going up half an octave as she declared, "No, nothing's wrong, Mr. Colton."

"You're sure?" he pressed, his dark eyes growing more so as he pinned her with a look.

The dark-haired woman squirmed, visibly uncomfortable under his close scrutiny.

"Yes, sir, I'm sure."

With that, Gloria picked up her pace and quickly hurried on her way.

Turning back around, Zane saw the look of distress pass over Mirabella's face just as the elevator arrived. He ushered her into the car and then followed behind. Through no fault of her own, she'd wound up a victim in this.

His first inclination was to protect her.

"Don't let it get to you," he advised in a hushed voice.

Mirabella raised her eyes to his just as the elevator door closed.

"How can I *not* let it get to me?" Mirabella wanted to know. "Gloria was condemning me. I could see it in her eyes when she looked at me. I've known her for *two years*," she underscored. "How can she be so willing to believe something so awful about me? About us?" Mirabella added, growing increasingly agitated. Her own words came echoing back to her and she realized what that had to imply. "I mean, there is no 'us,' but—" Mirabella stumbled, at a loss as to how to correct what she'd accidentally said. Helpless, she looked up at him. "You know what I mean, Mr. Colton."

Rather than just turn it into a joke or shrug it off, Zane felt for her.

"I know exactly what you mean and I know exactly what you're feeling," he assured her. "But this *will* blow over eventually."

Mirabella let out a breath. "I know that," she answered as they got off on the basement level. "People always find something else to talk about eventually. But the amount of damage that can be done between now and 'eventually…'"

Her voice trailed off, leaving it up to him to fill in the blanks.

Reaching his car, Zane pressed the button that simultaneously unlocked all the doors and then held the passenger door open for her.

"Give it a couple of days," he told Mirabella. Getting in on his side, he continued. "Just ignore the snide remarks."

"And what if, after a couple of days, it just continues or even gets worse?" she asked. "What then?"

"Then I'll think of something," Zane promised, putting his key into the ignition. The vehicle rumbled to life.

Listening to his advice, Mirabella nodded her head stoically and just stared straight ahead as he drove out of the parking garage and onto the street.

"I tried to be discreet," she said, beginning to speak quietly, as if she were just thinking out loud. "I mean, I couldn't help being sick all the time, but I'd always make sure there was no one else in the ladies' room to overhear me whenever I went in. And I didn't tell a soul about the baby," she said, lowering her voice to almost a whisper. "The only one who knew about it was my doctor."

Zane spared her a quizzical glance. She'd forgotten

someone—hadn't she? "How about the baby's father? Didn't you tell him?"

The laugh he heard didn't seem to belong to her. "Oh, I told him, all right. Trust me, he wouldn't have told anyone. He didn't even want to hear about it himself," she added bitterly. And then she shrugged. "Anyway, a couple of weeks after I told him, it wasn't an issue."

"I don't understand," he said, trying to make some sense out of the confusing comment. "Why wouldn't it be an issue?" When she made no effort to answer him, Zane made a guess. "Did he get married?"

She took a breath before answering. "Please, I really don't want to talk about it. It's over and I want to put it all behind me. The only thing you need to know is the baby's father isn't your stepfather. Beyond that, no disrespect intended, it's not any of your business."

"None taken," he replied, giving no indication how any of her rather anger-filled statement affected him.

Mirabella let out a shaky breath and ran her hand over her face as if that somehow helped pull herself together. She wasn't normally the type of person to have an outburst, or tell her boss to, in effect, back off.

She felt as if she was coming unglued.

"I'm sorry, sir, it's just been that kind of a day." She turned to look at him, clearly haunted by what was going on. "Why would whoever wrote that awful email even *think* that you, that I—that we would be sleeping together? You've never even *looked* at me like that and I've certainly never made any advances toward you. How could someone fabricate something like that completely out of nothing?" she wondered, feeling totally bewildered, not to mention helpless.

"Who knows what goes through someone's head?" he said with a dismissive shrug. "You'll make yourself crazy if you try to figure it out," he warned. "If you turn this around and somehow think you're responsible in some way for making this happen, you'll just be playing into that person's hands.

"Whoever did send that email was trying to get back at one of us, or stain our reputations for some reason that only he or she knows. The best way to make this go away is to just ignore it," he told her.

For once in her life, she wasn't that hopeful. What he was suggesting wasn't easy.

"What if it *doesn't* go away? What if it just gets worse?" Because she had this uneasy feeling it would.

"Then I'll handle it," he said again. "Just as I said I would. Nobody's going to hurt you, Belle. I won't let them," he promised.

She pressed her lips together, wishing she could believe that. Wishing she could take all of this as stoically as he did.

But she couldn't.

She wasn't the type to put blinders on and hold her head up while people around her hurled rocks and insults at her.

What she wanted to do was pick up those rocks and throw them right back at whoever had thrown them in the first place.

And then, after the dust settled and everyone had gone away, she'd burst into tears. But she'd do it privately, not where anyone could see her crying.

Struggling to get into Zane's frame of mind, Mirabella clenched her hands in her lap.

Zane pulled his vehicle up in front of Diego's, a family-owned Mexican restaurant he favored.

The establishment had been in the same location for the last twenty-three years and the building itself was sadly in need of a fresh coat of paint and a few minor repairs. But every dime of profit made was put back into the restaurant itself, into finding ways to make it even better than it already was.

The ingredients were always top quality and the food was always excellent.

Small, the restaurant was far off the beaten path, but its clientele was loyal and growing. And he was among them.

Zane wasn't sure just what had made him bring Mirabella here tonight, but he thought she might welcome the privacy and he was convinced she would enjoy the food.

"This is it," he announced, turning off his engine. "Let's go in."

Getting out, he rounded the hood and came around to her side.

He opened the passenger-side door for her, but instead of getting out, Mirabella just remained sitting in the passenger seat, looking at the restaurant. She noticed one of the lights on the far end, to her right, was out.

All she could think was this could pass for a secret hideaway in someone's estimation.

She looked at Zane. He was too smart not to realize that. "Isn't this doing just what that email implied we were doing?"

"What? Eating?" he asked.

Maybe he *didn't* realize it. Maybe, because he didn't

think this way himself, he was too close to all this to see the implications. "No, sneaking around."

"We're not 'sneaking around,'" he contradicted. "We're here in what *was* broad daylight when we started out." He nodded toward the restaurant. "Diego's isn't exactly on the beaten path, but it's not some secret den of iniquity, either." He didn't want her thinking he was deliberately trying to cut her off from people and bring her here for his own purposes. "I thought after what you've been through today, all of it," he emphasized, not minimizing his own part in it, "you deserve a little privacy and some really good food."

Maybe she was being hypersensitive and overreacting, Mirabella thought. Zane was just being considerate. She shouldn't be giving him a hard time over this.

It wasn't his fault the people in the office liked to gossip and if there was nothing to gossip about, they went out of their way to blow something out of proportion.

"Yes to the first part," she told him, letting him know she was grateful for some privacy, "but as for the second part, I'm not sure I can keep anything down except maybe crackers."

He took her protest in stride. "They're not on the menu, but I'm sure I can persuade Diego to just give you the taco shell without the ingredients that usually go inside." Then he smiled at her. "Diego's wife gave him six kids. If anyone knows about morning sickness, he does," he assured her.

Zane put his hand out to her. He was waiting for her to take it so he could help her out of the car if she needed it. But he didn't want her to feel pressured, so he waited in silence.

After a moment, Mirabella curled her fingers around his and allowed him to help her out of the vehicle. "Why are you being so nice?"

He had to remind himself to let go of her hand. It felt so natural in his, for a second he forgot he was holding it.

"I'm always nice," he quipped.

Mirabella inclined her head. "I mean, to me."

About to walk up to the entrance, he stopped and looked at her for a moment. She made it sound as if this behavior on his part was something new. "I don't recall having beaten you lately."

"You could have just told me not to worry about those awful emails and then gone home instead of bringing me here."

He didn't see it that way. "I accused you of some pretty awful things and no sooner do we clear that up and get it out of the way than you're bushwhacked by that email. You deserved a break and I owed you one," he told her simply.

Pausing, Zane offered her his arm. After a moment's hesitation, Mirabella took it.

And, with that one simple action, she lost her heart to him.

She sincerely doubted he realized it. She took great pains to appear totally unaffected by his gallant gesture. But kindness was not something she had ever taken for granted and she wasn't about to start now. While Mirabella wanted to believe the best of everyone, she was still enough of a realist—especially after being so unceremoniously abandoned by Kyle when he learned she was carrying his baby—to know evil existed out there.

And if, for some reason, that little fact would ever slip her mind in the future, all she had to do was recall that first awful, blistering email and she would most assuredly be reminded of that simple, unadorned fact of life.

Even if she didn't want to be.

Chapter 9

As she walked into the restaurant, Mirabella felt as if she were on the receiving end of a warm embrace delivered by her beloved grandmother. She couldn't quite explain why, but she could feel her tension leaving her body and slipping away. The homey atmosphere made her feel relaxed and at ease, the complete antithesis of what she'd felt during that last hour in the office.

A middle-aged woman—the owner's wife, Mirabella guessed—crossed to them, a genuinely welcoming smile on her kind, round face. Her dark eyes seemed to literally sparkle as she approached and regarded them.

Her hands outstretched, she shook Zane's hand between her own.

"Welcome back, Mr. Colton. It is always so good to see you here." Still smiling, the woman's expressive eyes shifted from Zane to his companion. "And you have brought someone new, I see." The corners of her eyes crinkled as her smile widened, this time focused entirely on Mirabella. "Welcome to Diego's, my dear," the woman said to her. "As it so happens, Mr. Colton, your usual table is free."

With that, the woman turned and led the way to a booth that was located toward the back of the room, off to one side. The older woman's ample hips swayed rhythmically as she walked ahead of them.

Stopping at the booth, she deposited two menus on the table and gestured for them to take their seats. "Dolores will be here in a moment to take your orders—unless you need some extra time," she qualified, addressing her words to Mirabella. "Mr. Colton, he knows the menu by heart," she added proudly.

"Thank you, Rita. We might need a few minutes," Zane responded.

The hostess nodded. "I will tell Dolores to take her time," she promised. Then, pausing for a moment, she looked at Zane with compassion in her dark eyes. "They will find him, Mr. Colton," she assured him with confidence. Then, flashing an encouraging smile at Mirabella, Rita withdrew.

"I guess you really *do* come here a lot," Mirabella commented.

Zane nodded. "I tend to stick with something I like," he replied.

Opening the rust-colored menu, Mirabella glanced over the two pages quickly. There were a number of dishes listed, but they all seemed to merge together before her eyes. The words *hot*, *spicy* and *fiery* seemed to spring up at her.

With a sigh, she closed the menu again, putting it back down on the table.

Zane raised a quizzical eyebrow. "What's wrong?"

There was no point in pretending what she saw on the menu wasn't at odds with her stomach. "I'm sure the food's very good here, but I'm really not up to eating anything hot or spicy."

"Then you won't," he replied simply. "The nice thing about Diego's is that Rita and her husband really *do* want to please their customers." Zane opened his menu, skimmed down both pages and found what he felt was a solution. "How does a grilled chicken burrito sound—without the cheese, refried beans or hot sauce?"

"Bland," Mirabella admitted. "And not why most people come to eat in a Mexican restaurant."

"That's one way to put it," he agreed. "I see it as protein you can consume and hopefully hold down." Zane set his menu down, still looking at his assistant. "And isn't that the main reason for you to eat right now? To take in good food that'll help nurture your baby?"

What he said made sense—as long as she could keep whatever she ate down.

"You have a point," she conceded, then hesitated. "Are you sure the chef won't be insulted if I ask to have the order changed from what's on the menu?"

Zane could only look at her in amused amazement. Mirabella was worried about hurting the feelings of someone she would probably never even meet. That placed her leagues above whoever had sent out that spiteful email, he thought. She was a really good person who deserved to be treated so much better than she had been today.

It made him ashamed of his own initially negative thoughts about her. He'd let the events get the better of him and he shouldn't have.

Zane found himself wanting to make it up to her somehow.

"I'm sure," he told her. He could see by her expression that Mirabella still had doubts. "Don't worry, I'll handle it," he promised.

She didn't want him going through any trouble—especially since there was another very real problem in the possible offing.

"Bland as it sounds, I'm not even sure I can keep that sauceless, cheeseless chicken down," she murmured.

He didn't see Mirabella as the timid type, but he could see where it might get rather embarrassing for her, having to make a sudden dash to the ladies' room. Still, she couldn't allow what *might* happen to dictate her actions.

"Well, we won't know unless we try, right?" he asked gamely as Dolores approached their booth to check on them.

"Are you ready to order?" the young woman asked in a friendly voice, her question sweeping over both of them. "Or do you still need a little more time?"

Glancing at Mirabella to make sure she was in agreement, Zane replied, "We're ready."

True to his word, he requested the proper modifications be made to her order. Mirabella expected some sort of a protest or reaction from the server, or, at the very least, to have Dolores roll her eyes. But neither happened. The young woman acted as if jotting down substitutions to items on the menu was the norm rather than the exception.

Finished taking down their orders, Dolores nodded smartly. "I'll be back with your dinners as soon as they're ready," she promised. "Until then, would either of you like something to drink?" She looked from one to the other, waiting.

Mirabella assumed the server was asking about alcoholic beverages and was about to demur when she heard Zane tell the young woman, "The lady will have some plain hot tea with lemon on the side. As for me, I'll have a lemonade."

Dolores flashed him a smile that transformed her face to a younger version of Rita's.

"Very good, Mr. Colton," the young woman commented just before she collected the two menus and withdrew from their booth.

He saw Mirabella looking at him quizzically and assumed it had something to do with how he'd taken the liberty of ordering for her.

"I thought the tea might help soothe your stomach," he explained.

The quizzical look on Mirabella's face only intensified. "How would you know that?" Pregnancy seemed to have a way of changing all the ground rules.

He laughed softly at her skepticism. "You're not the first person in the office to get pregnant," Zane told her, adding, "I observe things."

"Apparently," she murmured. The man seemed aware of a great many things that were going on around him, she couldn't help noticing. And then, remembering her manners, she tagged on a belated, "Thank you."

Zane shrugged off her gratitude. It was entirely unnecessary, and gratitude had always made him feel somewhat uncomfortable. He didn't do things to earn anyone's gratitude, he did them because he thought they needed doing.

"Don't mention it."

The server returned with their drinks and a round loaf of warm bread. The latter was perched on a cutting board along with more than enough butter to slather both sides of the loaf as well as every inch of its insides.

"So," Zane began conversationally once Dolores had retreated again, "what are you going to do?"

She thought he was referring to the very immediate situation.

"Try to eat the meal and see if it stays down," she said gamely. "It's the least I can do after you've gone through all this trouble for me."

Shaking his head, Zane smiled at her. "No, I mean about the baby."

The smile that was even now attempting to surface to her lips faded instantly as an alert look entered her eyes.

Was he asking her what she thought he was asking? Did he want to know if she was contemplating sweeping this baby from her life before she even saw it? Maybe she'd been wrong about him all along.

"It's *not* an inconvenience," she informed him tersely.

"I know," he replied quietly. Was that what she assumed he was thinking? "I didn't mean to imply in any way that I thought it was. I was just asking if you've made any plans on what to do once he or she was here?"

Mirabella blew out a breath. What was wrong with her head, anyway? Zane was being nothing but kind to her and she was getting all combative. He probably thought she was some psycho and he should be backing away posthaste.

"Right now," she told him honestly, "I'm just putting one foot in front of the other, trying to get through each day as it comes."

Zane tried to be clearer. "Do you have anyone who could help you?"

"What do you mean by 'help'?" She wanted to know.

Her mind kept jumping around from one thing to another like a giant frog trying to find a lily pad that suited him. Although she wanted to think the best, especially of Zane, she just couldn't help the fact that suspicion and distrust kept insisting on rearing its head, spoiling any shot she had at attaining peace of mind, or any sort of even semi-tranquility.

Rather than take offense at her tone, Zane patiently explained what he was asking her. "Do you have someone you're close to, someone you can talk to? You know, like family."

The word *family*, in the traditional sense, had ceased to mean things to her. But since she was expecting, it looked as if she was going to have to redefine her parameters, Mirabella thought.

Because he was still waiting for her to give him some sort of an answer, she proceeded slowly. "My parents are divorced and leading their own lives in different parts of the country." Her tone was stoic. "We were never close anyway," she added with a shrug.

She did have a grandmother who she adored. The woman had practically raised her, but this wasn't something Mirabella could bring to her. Her grandmother was very old-fashioned.

Raising her eyes to his, she said almost defensively, "I'll manage. Don't worry. I won't let it affect my work."

"I'm not worried about that," he told her, his voice mild as he cut a slice of the bread sitting between them. He offered the slice to her. "You might want to skip the butter," he suggested, nodding at the small ceramic vat next to the cutting board. "Otherwise it defeats the purpose."

"The purpose?" she echoed uncertainly.

He nodded. "It's crusty bread. Technically, white bread. That might help soothe your stomach."

Mirabella glanced at the cup beside her. "Like the tea," she guessed.

Zane smiled. "Like the tea. Now you're catching on," he said with approval.

"Not that I don't appreciate it," she qualified, "but why are you so concerned about me?" She thought of his missing stepfather. "Don't you have enough on your plate right now?"

"I do," he agreed, deliberately keeping his emotions in check. It was the only way he could deal with the situation. "But, aside from everything else at play here, for better or worse, you and I seem to be linked together in people's minds. At least in this case."

He was referring to that hateful email. She wondered if the tech Zane felt could perform acts of internet magic could somehow erase that email, and any comments it generated, off the server. She knew it would certainly make her happy.

"I didn't think you cared about what people thought," she said, surprised.

"Honestly, I don't," he replied. "But I'm not the only one involved in this," he said, looking at her significantly. "I don't really know all that much about you," he went on to admit, "but if you do need someone to talk to, you can always talk to me. This is a bad time to feel as if you're all alone."

The corners of her mouth curved ever so slightly. She had to stop being so suspicious of everything, Mirabella upbraided herself. Not everything had an ulterior motive behind it.

"I do appreciate that," she told him. "And if I bit your head off before, I truly am sorry. I'm afraid I haven't exactly been myself this last month or so," she apologized.

"Not 'bit,'" he replied, toning the situation down a little. "Nibbled on, maybe. And that's understandable," Zane was quick to add, absolving her of the blame she was so willing to heap on herself. "You've been dealing with a lot lately."

He was letting her off the hook. She knew she should just nod and agree, and be done with it. After all, Zane was being surprisingly more than nice, more than thoughtful, and she should just accept it as that. If she had any brains in that head of hers, Mirabella upbraided herself, she would.

But honesty was something she valued above all else and she felt she had to explain to Zane just why she seemed to be behaving so erratically.

"I feel like an old-fashioned yo-yo," she told him, searching for the right words.

Those were obviously not them.

She saw Zane's eyebrows draw together over the bridge of his nose as he obviously tried to relate what she was saying to the situation.

He failed.

"Come again?"

She put it a different way. "My emotions are all over the map. One second I feel like laughing, the next, I'm fighting not to dissolve into a puddle of tears. My stomach makes me feel absolutely miserable about three-quarters of the time. I find myself wanting to do all these things—and yet I'm too tired to wrestle even a flea—"

"I didn't know fleas were into wrestling," he commented, doing his best not to laugh at the image she'd created in his head.

"Luckily for me, they're not," she quipped, then grew serious again. "But what I'm trying to say is that I don't know if I'm coming or going. I always thought if the time ever came when I was pregnant, I'd just be thrilled and filled with anticipation—not moody and filled with anxiety," she told him, frowning not at Zane but at her own self-image.

"And I imagine that email didn't exactly help matters," he concluded as the server returned with their meals.

Mirabella made no comment on what he'd just said, but there was a frown on her lips that he took to be agreement.

He waited until after Dolores had told them both to "Enjoy," and then withdrew from the table.

When she did, he lowered his voice and told Mirabella, "I'm going to have Meyer trace whoever sent that email and they'll be made to publicly retract it and the sender will be disciplined." It wasn't what he wanted to do, but the email seemed to affect her so much, he wanted to get her name cleared.

She offered him a quick, grateful smile. He probably thought she was too obsessed with this.

"Please, don't concern yourself on my account. I'll ride it out." And then her smile slipped into her eyes. "I'm tougher than I look."

"I never doubted it."

She couldn't tell if he was saying that to her tongue in cheek or if he actually meant it.

But she had to admit that talking to him like this, being with him in such a welcoming atmosphere, went a long way toward making her feel better, at least for the time being.

She knew that tomorrow she'd be back at the office, facing whoever it was who had started this awful rumor and set it in motion—or, at the very least, she'd be suffering the consequences of that person's postings.

But for now, she made the conscious decision not to think about it. She might not be able to control everything, but she could, if she put her mind to it, control her own reaction to the circumstances that were affecting her life. She could either let those circumstances sweep her away, or she could stand her ground and make the best of it.

She chose to do the latter. It wasn't in her to go any other route.

Zane could see the change in her.

Mirabella seemed to brighten right in front of his eyes.

More hormones at play? he couldn't help wondering. Well, whatever it was, he had to admit it seemed to suit her. She especially had a really nice smile and she aimed it at him now. It was the kind of smile that wove itself into the main fabric of a person's consciousness, brightening their existence as it all but crept into their soul.

He glanced at Mirabella's bread dish and was happy to see it was empty. She'd finished eating the slice he'd cut for her without being aware of it.

Progress.

"Feeling better?" he asked conversationally.

For a second, she wasn't sure what Zane was referring to, and then she glanced down at her plate. The bread was gone and she'd started to eat dinner, all while they'd been talking.

She waited for her stomach to lurch in protest and was delighted when it didn't.

"Actually," she told him with a wide smile, "I think I am."

He nodded. "Told you the warm tea would do the trick."

No, Mirabella thought, *actually, it's not the tea. You're what did the trick.*

But she knew she couldn't say that, not without having Zane think she had some sort of designs on him, or wanted to turn this admittedly somewhat awkward situation to her advantage, though at the same time it would amount to his ultimate disadvantage.

So instead, she nodded and quietly replied, "Yes, you did," giving the appearance of agreeing with him.

Chapter 10

Zane thought it had died down.

No more salacious emails turned up on his computer from "Anonymous." Nor was he on the receiving end of any group emails sent en masse by any of the employees who felt compelled to take part in some self-righteous forum concerning the initial subject of the email.

Over the next few days, as he made his way through the office, Zane would occasionally notice one of the people who worked for him glancing his way with a curious expression on their face. It seemed to him as if those people were still somewhat undecided whether or not to believe the hateful words that had been in the group email. But since he was a Colton, as well as the man in charge, no one so much as cast a judgmental look in his general direction, much less said something that could be taken as a criticism or a sarcastic evaluation of his personal life.

Furthermore, there were no conversations that stopped when he entered the room, no furtive discourses abruptly ceased when someone saw him approaching. In short, there was no indication at all that the memory of the malicious email was still alive and covertly breeding.

Zane took that to mean it had all blown over, just as he'd told Mirabella it would. He felt greatly relieved it *was* over, more for Mirabella's sake than his own.

But it hadn't blown over.

The thought was the first thing that occurred to him when he walked into the company break room.

Having a sudden—and rather unexpected—craving for something really sweet, Zane decided to get something out of the vending machine. It was almost three, well past lunch and any company breaks. He expected to find the room empty.

It wasn't.

Mirabella was sitting at one of the tables, her back to the entrance, what appeared to be a container of hot tea clutched in her hands.

He'd noted her absence from her desk just before he decided to see if the vending machine had anything appetizing to offer.

"I was afraid you were in the ladies' room, being sick again," he told her casually as he fed the vending machine the proper amount of coins.

The coins created an almost melodic noise as they made their way through the machine, their contents registering.

Startled to hear his voice, Mirabella suppressed the

involuntary gasp that rose in her throat. Her hands tightened around the container. She had to restrain herself from squeezing.

"I'm sorry," she apologized, "I didn't know you were looking for me."

Her voice sounded oddly subdued and monotone, unlike her usual invigorated, animated tone. Zane chalked it up to Mirabella being tired. Lunch had long come and gone and he knew of a lot of people who experienced three-o'clock lag.

Being pregnant most likely made her more so.

"No harm done," he assured Mirabella. A tiny package of Oreo cookies fell off the spiral rack to the bottom of the machine. Pushing back the plastic partition, he retrieved his bounty. "I just need you to follow up on the report that was supposed to have come in regarding updating some of the surveillance cameras along the outer perimeter," he told her.

When she made no response, he paused at Mirabella's table. She still hadn't turned around, which he was beginning to think was rather odd.

"Belle? Did you hear what I just said?"

"Yes, yes I did," she answered, still apparently staring at a spot on the back wall. "You want me to track down the whereabouts of the McCay report," she said, referring to the report by name.

Well, Mirabella had apparently been listening, he thought, but something else was bothering him at this point.

There was obviously something wrong.

Since she wasn't turning around to look at him, he circled the small table for two until he was able to face her. Mirabella quickly lowered her head, but it was too late, he'd already seen what she was clearly attempting to hide from him.

Still holding the unopened packet of cookies in his hand, Zane sat down opposite her. Cocking his head, he peered into her face.

And then he understood why she was trying to avoid him.

"Belle," he addressed her gently, asking a question he already knew the answer to, "have you been crying?"

"No," she mumbled, still attempting to keep her head down.

Reaching across the table, Zane crooked his forefinger under her chin and raised it until he was able to get a better look at her face.

"If you haven't been crying, then why are your cheeks wet?"

"Allergies," she told him evasively. "I've been sneezing."

"Oh? Then where's your handkerchief?" Zane challenged.

"I used tissues," she answered stubbornly. "They're disposable."

"Also apparently invisible," he commented. Reaching into his pocket, he took out his handkerchief and handed it to her. After a moment's hesitation, she took it. "Talk to me, Belle," he requested.

Wiping her eyes, Mirabella raised her head to look at him. "Why do you call me that?" she asked, trying to distract him. "Everyone else calls me by my full name." Although, if anyone had asked her, she had to admit she rather liked the nickname he'd given her.

"Your name's too long," he told her matter-of-factly.

"And I've already wasted enough time. Now, what happened?" he asked.

His tone was kind, but at the same time, he was making it very clear to her that he wasn't about to tolerate any lies. He wanted the truth.

Mirabella felt stupid having to explain herself. He had too much to handle already without having to listen to her. But he was waiting, so she finally told him in a small, lost voice, "I was disinvited."

"Disinvited?" he questioned, not sure what she meant.

Mirabella sighed. He wanted the whole story, so she gave it to him.

"All right." She raised her head and looked at him, allowing her complete distress to show through. "If you insist on knowing, I was *fired*."

He still didn't understand what she was talking about.

"No, you weren't," he contradicted. "You work for me. That means no one can fire you from here except for me—and I haven't."

"Not from here," she told him, obviously struggling not to cry again. "I was fired from the Clothe the Children Foundation's annual benefit party. I was on the planning committee," she explained. Mirabella pressed her lips together to keep her voice from cracking before continuing. "The chairwoman called to say she'd been 'made aware' of 'certain goings-on' and they don't need that sort of attention drawn to their organization. She thanked me for my past efforts and told me that I was no longer needed there."

Mirabella raised her eyes to his again. "I've been part of that foundation for almost five years now.

Working on it meant a great deal to me. And they let me go just like that. Tossed me away like a used envelope," she added, crushed.

Zane had never seen anyone looking as disheartened, as distressed, as Mirabella did right at this very moment. His heart went out to her, wanting to protect her, to make things right.

"What's her name?" He wanted to know. "The chairwoman, what's her name? I'll make a call."

But Mirabella shook her head. She didn't want him fighting her battles for her.

"I doubt it would do any good," she said. "But thanks for the offer." Handing him back his handkerchief, she did her best to smile at him. The effort was weak and heart tugging.

"I thought all this had died down," Zane said, tucking away his handkerchief.

Her lips twisted in a smile that didn't even come near reaching her eyes. But rather than bitterness, all he saw there was sorrow.

"Oh, it hasn't," she assured him, then amended, "At least, not for me. Whoever is behind this, what do they get out of it?" she wondered for the umpteenth time. "What does he or she get out of making me feel so miserable?"

"You shouldn't feel miserable," Zane told her. "You're still the same person you were before whoever it is started spreading all these lies."

But Mirabella just shook her head. He was wrong. This had left a mark on her. A dark mark.

"Not to hear the way other people talk," she confided. "They think I had this coming for putting on airs."

He looked at her, at a loss as to what to make of what she'd just said. She was the most unassuming person he knew. "What airs?"

Mirabella merely shrugged in response. "I don't know," she said honestly, "but that seems to be the prevailing opinion around here lately. Everyone thinks I'm having your baby and bilking your father's bank account to finance my decadent life from here on in. When I overheard one of them say that and pointed out I'm still here, working, I was told it's just for appearances—until after the baby's born."

Mirabella pressed her lips together, staring at the top of the tea in her container, watching the overhead light break up on the surface of the hot liquid and become distorted.

It was a metaphor, she thought, for her life.

She let out a long, shaky breath before telling him, "I don't want to hand in my resignation."

Zane looked at her sharply. Where had *that* come from? "Who said anything about handing in your resignation?"

Her eyes shifted to his. There were fresh tears shining in them again. She struggled to keep them from falling.

"It's the only way I can get this to stop," she explained. "The only way I can get everyone to stop gossiping and spreading lies about me—about you," she added in a small voice.

"Don't worry about me," he ordered. An idea occurred to him and he debated saying anything for a moment, then decided to go for it. "There is another way you can get them to stop spreading lies."

"What other way?" she asked, her hand resting protectively on her stomach.

Was he going to tell her to get rid of her baby? No, she refused to believe that, refused to believe he could be that unfeeling.

But then, she wouldn't have believed so many of the people she worked with could have turned on her like this, either. And they had. With a vengeance in some cases.

"You could marry me."

Mirabella's mouth dropped open. She stared at Zane in absolute stunned silence. And then she shook her head, certain she had misheard him.

"I am really getting delusional," she half laughed. "For a second, I thought I heard you say I could marry you."

Zane moved in a little closer. Now that he'd said it out loud, it just seemed like it was the right solution. He didn't know why it had taken him this long to come up with it.

"You did. I did. You can."

She could only continue to stare at him in utter disbelief.

"You're serious," she cried.

He didn't see the problem. Why was she having so much trouble accepting this? Had he been wrong about the attraction he thought was between them? "Why wouldn't I be?"

"Well, for one thing," she began to enumerate, "it's insane. For another, you don't love me."

Too late, Mirabella realized she hadn't phrased that properly. What she should have said was that *they* didn't love each other. But she had isolated it to just him who didn't love in this case. Had he picked up on the fact that she'd slipped, inadvertently letting him know how she felt about him?

Mirabella held her breath, watching his face for some sign of a sudden dawning of facts occurring.

A moment passed and he apparently had no such epiphany—thank God!

Instead, he calmly informed her, "That doesn't matter."

Did he really believe that? It sounded so cold, it made her heart ache. "Love matters," she insisted.

Zane tried again. He absolutely hated seeing her suffer like this without being able to do something about it.

His reaction had taken him somewhat by surprise, but with everything that had been going on lately— this, not to mention his father's abduction—the state of his emotions was in an entire upheaval and he couldn't make heads or tails of anything.

"I'm not saying it doesn't," Zane insisted, "but look at it logically. Everyone thinks this is my baby anyway. If you don't marry me, you're going to wind up being a single mother with a ruined reputation and an unhappy baby. Is that the sort of world you want to bring your baby into? The kind of life you want your baby condemned to?"

When he put it that way, she felt as if she was being selfish. "No, but—"

He overrode her protest and outlined his plan for them. "We'll get married and then after the baby is born and it has my name, we'll let a suitable amount of time pass, then cite that old saw, *irreconcilable differences*, and get divorced. After that, I'll set you and the baby up with a comfortable monthly allowance and we'll each go our own way. Problem neutralized." He could see he'd caught Mirabella completely off guard. He didn't want to seem as if he was pressuring her, but to him, it did seem like the perfect solution. "Think about it," he urged. "It's the best thing for everyone. The baby gets a father, you can stop fending off insults and lies—"

"And what do you get out of it?" Mirabella asked. She didn't think of him as a selfish person, but most people didn't just selflessly go out of their way like this, fixing what was apparently a wrong in their eyes.

"Me?" Zane answered her with a smile, something, she took note of, that didn't happen very often. "I get back a fully functional administrative assistant I depend on possibly way too much, but it's too late to change that. So, what do you say?"

She already knew what she was going to say, even though it pained her to do so.

"No."

He looked at her, dumbfounded. He was considered to be one of the state's most eligible bachelors. Getting women had never been a problem for him. Fighting them off had been the real problem. Yet Mirabella had just turned down his proposal in less than a heartbeat. Why?

"No?"

"No," she repeated. Taking a breath, she searched for the right words. There really weren't any, but she had to try. "Mr. Colton—"

Zane permitted himself a guarded smile. She did amuse him. "Under the circumstances, I think you can call me Zane."

Mirabella inclined her head. "All right, *Zane*. I appreciate everything you're trying to do for me, I really do," she said without hesitation, "but I am not going to get married because it's the *practical* thing to do and I'm not going to allow a bunch of catty, jealous people who have nothing better to do but tear someone down for entertainment purposes push me into a corner like this. I know you mean well, Mr.—Zane, and it's all very kind of you. But as far as I'm concerned, there is only one reason and one reason alone that one person marries another person and that's because they love each other."

"A lot of monarchs throughout history might have taken exception to that," Zane pointed out.

A small, sad smile played on her lips. "There are no kingdoms involved here, Zane. Or, at least, I don't have one to my name," she amended.

He failed to understand what she was driving at. "Meaning, I do?"

He had to ask? "The name Colton around here means power," she reminded him. "Your father built an empire out of next to nothing."

Zane thought of some of the stories he'd heard growing up, both from his mother when she married Eldridge and from the man himself later on. The road to building up that so-called empire had not been a straight one, nor had it always been a strictly honest one. There were dealings he'd heard Eldridge had looked back on with some regret and remorse, now that all was said and done.

But they weren't talking about his father's eligibility for canonization to sainthood, they were talking about something Zane viewed as the most practical approach to a very annoying problem.

"It's called a marriage of convenience for a reason," he told her.

"Maybe," Mirabella allowed. "But I don't see what you're suggesting as a convenience. I see it as nothing more than a lie."

It occurred to him that he had never met anyone quite like Mirabella before. Usually, everyone was just out for themselves. She seemed to be out for everyone *except* herself.

"Think of your baby," he reminded her.

"I am thinking of the baby," she told him. "And I don't want him or her to ever discover they had been born into a lie."

Genuinely surprised by her reasoning, Zane looked at her. "So it's a no?" he asked Mirabella, giving her one last chance to change her mind.

"It's a no," she confirmed. Standing up, Mirabella squared her shoulders. "Now, if you'll excuse me, my boss wants me to track down a report and I don't like to disappoint him."

Zane rose from the table as well, joining her as they walked out of the break room. He was seeing her in a brand-new light, and that light was very flattering. She was a fighter. He liked that.

"I really don't think that's possible, Belle," he told her quietly.

Chapter 11

Mirabella told herself it didn't matter. That she was stronger than she'd thought and that, digging deep for inner strength, she could bear up to anything. She sought comfort in the idea that Zane was right. Everything, good or bad, eventually blew over and this would, too.

Eventually.

All she had to do was wait out the storm.

And maybe, if she was really as alone as she'd indicated to Zane, in an odd sort of way, she could just continue ignoring the whispers, the snide remarks and the barely veiled insults that kept coming her way.

But she wasn't completely alone. While she'd told him the truth that both her parents were now elsewhere, living their lives with their spouses, there was one very dear person in her life who mattered a great deal to her. One person she would do anything to protect, to shield and do anything to ensure she wasn't hurt—and that person was her beloved grandmother. Sofia Sanchez, the sweet, rock of a woman who had always been there for Mirabella during her childhood, had been the one who had shielded her.

When what seemed like daily battles broke out between her parents, Sofia, her mother's mother, had been her haven. Living close by, the older woman would invite her to stay with her when things became particularly intolerable at home. During those days, the small, animated woman provided the much-needed stability missing from the life she had with her parents.

Wrapped up in their own minidramas, her parents hardly noticed her. In those rare times when they *did* notice her, she became the object of a tug-of-war between them, made to feel like an object rather than a person with real feelings.

Even then, her grandmother didn't take sides. Sofia always assured her that her parents loved her. She told her that they were just two very unhappy, mismatched people who had no real idea how to live harmoniously. Instead of taking a negative view of things, her grandmother always told her to be patient, that things would eventually calm down and work themselves out.

Sofia also told her to always remember she was loved, by her parents and, very fiercely, by her.

"What would you think of me now, Nana?" Mirabella asked as she looked herself over in the mirror just before she got dressed. She still wasn't showing, but she could well envision what she would look like, rounded out with a child. "If you knew about this baby, would you stop loving me?"

She couldn't bear the thought of that happening, so she had been putting off the inevitable. Putting off telling her kind, sweet, diminutive grandmother that she had gotten pregnant because one night, she had too much to drink and became vulnerable and careless.

"Would you disown me?" Mirabella questioned the woman who was there only in spirit. "Would you just walk away, shaking your head?"

Sofia Sanchez was a wonderful, kind, loving woman who had taught her to always share what she had. If her grandmother had only one loaf of bread and saw someone hungry, she would gladly give them half. It was a philosophy that was well rooted, as were all of her values.

They were also old-fashioned. And because Sofia had old-fashioned values, her grandmother believed a young woman should be married before she ever knew any pleasures of the flesh, much less before she became pregnant.

Good girls wait, Mirabella, her grandmother had told her more than once. *It is not easy*, Sofia had admitted understandingly. *But they wait. That is why it is so much more precious when you give yourselves to one another.*

"Precious" is off the table, Nana, Mirabella thought with a sigh.

Each time she picked up the telephone to call her grandmother, she could hear her grandmother's voice in her head, talking about priorities, about *saving* herself until after marriage.

And each time, she let the receiver drop back into the cradle, promising herself that she would call her grandmother, soon.

Her grandmother had to know something was wrong, Mirabella silently argued. Sofia wasn't a fool. Using one excuse or another, she hadn't been to see her grandmother in close to two months. But with each day that passed by, maintaining the lie was becoming too huge a burden for her to bear. However, she knew that although she still wasn't showing, something she said or did in her grandmother's company was bound to give her secret away.

And so, she continued to put off a face-to-face meeting. Her grandmother would call, inviting her over, saying she hadn't seen her in what felt like a very long time, and she would tell her grandmother she had to go out of town on business, or she was working overtime, helping Zane with a security overhaul, and wouldn't be able to make it over in the foreseeable future.

She said anything and everything—except for the truth.

She was behaving like a coward, Mirabella angrily upbraided herself. Hiding didn't become her, nor was it anything she had ever done before this situation had cropped up. If nothing else, her grandmother deserved better than that.

So, summoning bits and pieces of her tattered courage, on the following Sunday afternoon, Mirabella drove over to her grandmother's house. She nearly turned back twice, but somehow, giving herself mental pep talks, she managed to finally get there.

Standing on the familiar doorstep to her grandmother's house, Mirabella held her breath and rang the bell. When there was no response, she tried again, wondering if she should have called first to make sure her very active grandmother was home—although, up to this point, her grandmother had *always* been home. It was one of the rare, stable things in life she felt she could rely on.

When there was no immediate response to her ringing the doorbell again, Mirabella decided it was an omen. Feeling almost relieved, she was about to turn away when the door opened.

So much for a hasty retreat.

Her grandmother looked at her in surprise. "Mirabella, why didn't you use your key?"

Mirabella shrugged weekly. "I didn't want to just barge in on you," she said.

Sofia looked at her as if she couldn't process what her granddaughter was saying.

"Strangers barge, Mirabella. You are my granddaughter. Granddaughters don't barge," she maintained firmly. "Come in, come in," Sofia urged, all but pulling her inside. "I was just on the phone and I didn't want to be rude," she said, explaining why it had taken her so long to come to the door.

"I'm sorry, I didn't mean to interrupt," Mirabella apologized.

Sofia waved away the apology. "This woman, you can feel free to interrupt." And then she smiled broadly, focusing on her granddaughter. "Let me look at you," Sofia requested, taking her granddaughter's hands in hers and spreading them to get a better look at the young woman. "You look paler," she pronounced, releasing her hands.

Mirabella expected her grandmother to express concern and then question her about her eating habits. Instead, Sofia turned on her heel and led the way back into her kitchen.

Even before entering the kitchen, Mirabella could detect the enticing aroma of a pie baking in the oven. The very scent of it catapulted her back to her childhood, eagerly waiting for her grandmother to remove the pie from the oven.

For a moment, it felt as if nothing had changed. Except that *everything* had changed.

Gesturing for Mirabella to sit, Sofia took the pie out of the oven and placed it on top of the stove to cool for a moment.

"How long as it been?" she asked, her back still to Mirabella.

"How long has what been?" Mirabella asked uneasily, all her thoughts immediately converging on her condition. Was that what her grandmother was asking her about? How long she'd been pregnant? But how would the woman have known?

"Since I saw you last," Sofia said, turning around. "It feels like it's been months and months."

Mirabella offered her a smile. "It hasn't been that long, Nana."

Though she rarely sat, choosing to move about her kitchen like an echo in perpetual motion, Sofia sat down at the table and faced her granddaughter.

"Talk to me," she coaxed. Her voice was as kind as ever, but there was a slight note of urgency in it.

Or maybe that was just her guilty conscience, Mirabella thought, creating scenarios that didn't really exist.

"I know I should have come by for a visit sooner," she began, not certain where she was going with her excuse, only knowing she needed to at least attempt to tender some sort of explanation for her prolonged absence.

"Yes," Sofia agreed. "You should have." She glanced over her shoulder toward the stovetop. "Would you like some pie?" she offered.

Mercifully, Mirabella had begun to actually keep some of the things she ate down, but she didn't want to risk a possible bout of misplaced morning sickness right now, not while attempting to gently broach the subject to her grandmother.

So, as tempting as having one of her grandmother's pies really was, she felt it was safer to pass on having a slice right now.

"Maybe later," she demurred.

To which Sofia responded with, "Hmm," and made no further effort to push a piece of pie on her. Instead, she sat back in her chair, looking directly at her granddaughter for a long moment as if sorting her thoughts and prioritizing them.

Finally, leaning over the kitchen table, she took hold of her granddaughter's hand in hers. "You know you can come to me with anything, yes?" she asked, still looking at her face intently.

Mirabella drew in her breath, bracing herself just in case. "I know."

Sofia shook her head sadly. "And still, you don't."

Panic made a sudden, unexpected appearance, squeezing her heart as well as twisting her stomach. For a moment, her mind went completely blank.

The next moment, she heard herself protesting, rather unconvincingly, "That's not true."

Sofia fixed her with a penetrating look. "We have

never lied to one another, Mirabella. Please don't start now."

There was sadness in the woman's eyes and Mirabella didn't know if it was because her grandmother thought she was lying to her, or if there was something even bigger going on.

"Nana?" she asked uncertainly, waiting for the woman to explain why she thought she was lying.

"I was on the phone with Maria Montez when you rang the bell," Sofia began.

Her grandmother said the woman's name as if she was familiar with her, Mirabella shook her head. "I'm sorry, Nana. I don't know who that is."

Sofia waved her hand as if that fact was of no real consequence to the crux of this conversation. "Maria is just a woman I know. A woman who likes to talk and be the first to tell people things she believes they would be interested in hearing. Though she tries to cover them with her hair, her ears are very big," Sofia confided, "so she doesn't miss anything. To get to the point, Maria has a friend who has a cousin whose daughter works in the same building as you do." She paused significantly, waiting for the words to sink in.

The silence stretched out and Mirabella desperately wanted to apologize, to say she knew she'd disappointed her. But just in case she was overthinking this and her grandmother was going to say something entirely different at the conclusion, Mirabella waited, holding her breath.

Waited until there was no doubt left.

"Did you think I would stop loving you?" Sofia asked in a quiet voice.

There were tears glistening in her grandmother's

eyes. Tears that, Mirabella thought guiltily, she had put there.

"No matter what, you will always be my Mirabella," Sofia insisted, taking her granddaughter's hand. "No matter what you have done, you will always be my granddaughter and I will always love you and be there for you. Do you understand this?"

Mirabella could feel tears gathering in her own eyes. "Oh, Nana, I'm so sorry."

"I know you are, darling," Sofia told her. Getting up, she crossed to Mirabella and gathered her granddaughter in her arms, hugging her. For a small woman, she was surprisingly strong. After a moment, she looked down at her granddaughter and asked, "The father, he won't marry you?"

It was on the tip of Mirabella's tongue to blurt out the whole story, how Kyle had rejected her and then how shortly afterward he had died in a car accident. But what was the point of that? It would only make her grandmother sadder and there was no reason to further burden the woman.

The hurt she saw in her grandmother's eyes was already more than she could bear.

So instead of unburdening herself the way she had done so many times as a child, Mirabella told the older woman what she felt Sofia needed to hear in order for the woman to achieve at least some sort of peace of mind.

"He asked me, Nana, but I didn't want him to feel he had to." Which was true, although it hadn't been the baby's father who had asked her but the person everyone presumed was the baby's father.

Sofia looked at her in surprise. "Mirabella, these

are very modern times. Men don't do anything they don't want to do. There are still some honorable men around, but unfortunately, they are few and far between. If your baby's father wants to marry you, then *let* him marry you. Don't be stubborn, darling. You owe this to the baby you are carrying," she emphasized, searching Mirabella's eyes to see if her granddaughter understood.

After a moment, Mirabella capitulated. "You're right," she agreed.

Sofia rose from her chair and paused to kiss the top of her granddaughter's head. "Of course I am," she agreed. "Now will you have that pie?"

"Yes, please," Mirabella said with a smile.

Inside, Mirabella could feel her heart quickening. Now that she had come out and told her grandmother about Zane's proposal, she couldn't very well take back what she had said. Her grandmother was going to expect her to get married.

The problem was that even though Zane had asked her, would he still be willing to go through with it? After all, she had already turned him down. Not once, but twice, in quick succession.

She could do far worse than marry someone like Zane, even temporarily. He'd already impressed her that he was a good, decent man capable of thinking of someone else even though his own life was in a state of emotional chaos.

But that didn't necessarily mean he would be willing to marry her if she told him that she had changed her mind about her answer.

She looked up at her grandmother as Sofia placed a plate with a warm slice of pie on it in front of her.

She couldn't hurt this woman twice. No matter what, she was going to have to convince Zane Colton that she had changed her mind and was, despite her stand about a loveless marriage, ready to take him up on his generous offer.

Leaving her grandmother's house several hours later, Mirabella rehearsed what she was going to say to Zane over and over again in her head as she drove home.

The words, not to mention themes and variations of those words, had echoed countless times in her brain by the time she pulled up in her driveway.

Walking in, she dropped her purse by the front door and went straight to her landline instead of using her cell phone to call Zane. The last thing she wanted was to have her call suddenly wink in and out, or worse, get dropped in the middle of her rehearsed little speech.

Her palms felt damp as she pushed the numbers on the keypad to Zane's home phone.

She was so nervous, she misdialed the first time and wound up connecting to someone's fax machine by the sound of the high-pitched noise. Swallowing a mild curse, she pulled herself together and tried again.

This is for Nana, not for you, she told herself, squelching the urge to hang up before she got through.

This time, she hit the right numbers.

She heard Zane's deep voice against her ear. It sent tiny, warm shock waves all through her.

"Hello?"

Mirabella would have known his voice anywhere.

Her throat all but closed up on her. It took effort and willpower to force the word out. But there was far more than just her reputation at stake. This was about her grandmother's feelings. No matter what her personal feelings about doing this were, she couldn't allow herself to let that wonderful woman down any more than she already had.

"Yes!"

Chapter 12

Zane was fairly certain he recognized the voice and knew who was calling, but ever mindful of possible entrapment, either by the sheriff or someone working against him in his own company, he decided to take no chances and asked, "Belle?"

Idiot. You should have identified yourself first, she thought. She'd gotten so wound up in changing her answer, everything just seemed to have flown out of her head.

"Yes, it's me," Mirabella said.

"What were you saying yes to?" Zane asked.

Mirabella already felt like a fool, but she'd called him, so she had to explain what she was talking about—and why she would be disturbing his Sunday evening this way. And then it suddenly occurred to her, in the midst of all this, that she might very well be throwing a monkey wrench into his plans for that evening. What if he was with someone? In that case, he wasn't going to take this call kindly, never mind what she was agreeing to—*if* she could still agree to it and he hadn't changed his mind.

Maybe she shouldn't have called, Mirabella thought, having second thoughts.

"I'm not interrupting anything, am I?" she asked abruptly.

"Are you all right, Belle?" Zane asked her, concerned. "You seem a little...scattered," he finally said for lack of a better word.

Scattered was the last word he would have used to describe her in the past. Mirabella hadn't even come off that way in the beginning stages of her pregnancy, when she kept running off to the ladies' room right in the middle of things. All in all, she was the most centered, the most focused person that he knew.

"Sorry," she apologized quietly.

"Don't be sorry," he told her. "Just tell me what's going on. You're not experiencing any sort of an emergency, are you?"

Zane had no idea how to clearly phrase what he was actually asking without sounding as if he was getting too personal. He didn't feel he was really on that sort of footing with her, despite the years they had worked together.

Mirabella thought of her grandmother and of what she was about to do in order for the woman to be able to hold her head up again. To her, the situation was an emergency, but it wasn't the kind she knew he meant. She was just employing emergency measures in order to repair her reputation for her grandmother's sake.

"Only in the very broadest sense," Mirabella admitted. She knew that couldn't have cleared up anything for Zane, so she tried again. "I know it's been a couple of days since you made that generous gesture, but if the offer to marry you is still on the table, then my answer is yes."

She held her breath, waiting for Zane's response, hoping she hadn't destroyed her chances by attempting to stick to her principles, especially in light of the fact that she had allowed most of her principles to crumble to pieces by winding up in this condition in the first place.

After what seemed like an eternity, she heard Zane ask, "What changed your mind?"

Her heart sank. She'd let her one opportunity slip through her fingers. Zane was drawing this out, possibly out of curiosity, possibly to pay her back for rejecting him—men didn't take rejection well, she knew that firsthand. The bottom line was he wasn't telling her the offer was still good, that yes, they could get married.

Well, what did she expect? Mirabella angrily chastised herself. The offer had been too good to be true in the first place. She would have never dreamed he would have gone to such lengths to help her. But instead of jumping at it like a normal person, she had turned him down.

Still, he had asked her a question just now and because of what he had been willing to do for her, he did deserve an answer.

"My grandmother," she told him.

He took his time, as if he was stitching together her answers and trying to make sense of them. "She told you to marry me?"

"No," Mirabella said quickly, not wanting him to think her grandmother was some sort of an aged gold digger. "She doesn't even know you're the one who proposed to me. Up until today, she didn't even know I was pregnant—at least, I didn't think she knew because I hadn't told her and I hadn't been to visit her for two months," she added even more quickly. This wasn't coming out right. In her hurry to get everything on the table, allowing him to have all the facts, it was coming out a jumbled mess.

She wasn't accustomed to tripping over her own tongue, she thought in frustration.

From the way Mirabella had talked, he'd gotten the impression that, aside from estranged parents, she had no other family.

"I didn't realize you still had a grandmother. I take it the two of you aren't close." He'd made the assumption based on what she'd just told him, that she hadn't visited the woman in a while.

"No, that's just it," Mirabella contradicted, "we are. I didn't go to see her in those two months because I just didn't know how to break the news to her that I was pregnant."

Maybe he was missing something. "Most grandmothers want to become great-grandmothers," Zane said. "I hear it's a competitive thing. Yours doesn't?" he guessed, thinking there had to be a reason for her grandmother's negative attitude.

"Oh, she wants to be one very much." Mirabella sighed. "What she doesn't want is a pregnant, *unmarried* granddaughter."

The light went off in his head. Now it was beginning to make sense. "I see."

There was nothing in Zane's voice to tell her whether he did or not, or what he thought about the matter. But, since he wasn't terminating the call, she continued talking, hoping maybe he'd still be willing to go through this marriage charade.

"My grandmother more or less raised me when my parents' marriage began disintegrating. She was always warm and loving and she made me feel safe, especially when all hell was breaking loose on the home front." Mirabella paused for a second, wanting to phrase this just right. She didn't want him thinking her grandmother was this judgmental, shriveled up old lady. "My grandmother is also somewhat old-fashioned by today's standards."

Zane was beginning to see the light. "No babies before marriage," he guessed.

"No *anything* before marriage," Mirabella corrected philosophically.

"Oh." He found himself feeling sorry for Mirabella—again. "So how did she take the news?" He wanted to know. "About the baby?"

Mirabella could feel tears stinging her eyes again. She blinked them away. There was no point in crying over this. What was done was done.

"She told me that she still loved me." Her voice quavered a little. "But I knew she was disappointed."

"In you?" That didn't exactly sound very warm and loving to him.

"No, in the situation," Mirabella replied. "And then she asked me if the baby's father wasn't willing to marry me."

The pieces finally all came together. "And you said he was."

Which was why she was calling, he thought. Not because she'd changed her mind and wanted to marry *him*, but because she wanted to please her grandmother. It put somewhat of a different spin on everything.

She nodded before she realized he had no way of seeing her. "I told her that I'd turned you down because I didn't want you feeling obligated to marry me, just because of the baby." Mirabella sighed again, hating the deception she was forced to be part of, yet at the same time grateful to Zane for helping her—provided he was still willing to help her. "That was when she said I had an obligation to the baby to provide it with a two-parent home and not to allow my own stubbornness to get in the way of that."

"So, she knows you can be stubborn," she heard Zane say with a laugh. For a second, she allowed the sound to wrap itself around her, comforting her. And then she heard him ask in a more serious voice, "Does she know it's not mine?"

"I didn't mention you by name," she told him. "She just thinks the father of my baby was the one who asked me to marry him."

"And that's why you're calling," he concluded.

"That's why I'm calling." There was silence on the other end. Every second it continued, she became progressively more uneasy and much less sure she should have called at all. Finally, unable to take it, she blurted out, "Look, this was a bad idea. I'm sorry to have bothered you."

"What'll you tell your grandmother?" he asked, keeping her from hanging up.

"I'll think of something," she muttered. Right now, she couldn't think about that. "It's not your problem, sir."

"You're going to have to stop that, you know," Zane said.

She didn't understand. "Stop what?"

"Well, if we're going to be married, you can't keep calling me *sir*."

Was he saying he was willing to go through with it, after all? "Mr. Colton—"

"Or that," Zane pointed out. "This isn't the early 1900s when married couples referred to one another by their titles and surnames. That's one old-fashioned habit that has happily fallen by the wayside."

This was happening too fast for her. Thoughts were whizzing in and out of her head, jumbling in the process. "Wait, are you telling me that you still intend to marry me?"

"I thought we cleared that part up already," Zane said. "You *were* the one who just called to say yes, weren't you?"

"I was, I mean, I am." She was doing it again, tripping over her own tongue. Mirabella took a breath, trying to sound coherent. "It's just when you didn't say the offer was still open—"

None of this was coming out right, Mirabella thought, frustrated with herself. She closed her eyes, doing her best to get a grip on herself, not to mention on the situation.

After a moment, she tried again.

"When?"

"Give me a second," Zane replied.

There was some background noise as he checked what she presumed was an electronic calendar.

A minute later, he was back. "I've got meetings scheduled Monday and Tuesday." The information, he knew, was rhetorical since Mirabella was more familiar with his daily schedule than he was. "How about Wednesday?" he posed.

"Wednesday?" she echoed, suddenly feeling as if she had been propelled into some sort of a parallel universe or at the very least a dream world. Was he asking her to consider Wednesday as a day for their wedding?

To even *think* that felt so strange, she thought.

"For the wedding," he deliberately stressed in case she missed the point of this discussion. "Unless you can't get away," he qualified.

"I can get away," she answered, the words all but bursting out of her mouth before he could change his mind. And then reality hit her with an overwhelming force. "You want to get married that soon?" she asked in disbelief. Her head was beginning to spin from the very idea of all this actually coming together and becoming a reality.

"Why not?" He wanted to know. "There's no reason to wait if we've both agreed to set this marriage in motion, right?"

This sounded much too whirlwind for her tastes. Zane was forgetting things. "Aren't there arrangements that have to be made?" she questioned.

"You mean like for a big wedding?" he asked. "Is that what you want?"

What she wanted, Mirabella reasoned sadly, was for Zane to *really* want to marry her, not to save the day, but to do so because he loved her.

Take what you can get and stop whining, a little

.voice in her head ordered. *You're damn lucky he's actually offering to do this.*

"No," Mirabella said out loud, doing what she could to block out the inner voice driving her crazy. "Like for licenses and blood tests and things like that. We need time for that."

"You'd be right—if we were getting married here," Zane agreed. "But we can take the corporate jet and fly to Las Vegas." The plane was at his disposal, as it was for his father and several other executive officers within the company. "The whole thing can take under four hours, start to finish."

Her lips twisted in an ironic smile as she thought over his description. That didn't sound like much of a wedding day to her.

"That puts a whole new meaning to the term *dream wedding*. Blink and you sleep right through it," Mirabella quipped.

Everyone wanted someone at their wedding, he realized. Someone they cared about to witness the ceremony. "We could fly a few people out—your grandmother," he suggested. "Make it seem more festive."

"No, your way is better," she told him stoically. It was bad enough she was going to be lying to her grandmother—and continue lying until she and Zane finally got divorced and went their separate ways. She didn't want to have the woman participating in the charade, as well. "No muss, no fuss, no meetings missed."

"Belle—" he began to apologize, feeling that despite her cheerful flippancy, beneath it all, her feelings had somehow been hurt.

Didn't Mirabella realize he was attempting to shield her as best he could? That he'd only suggested this marriage to protect her, not himself? He'd been living on the cusp of a scandal all of his life, right from the moment his mother had first laid eyes on Eldridge Colton. A few more rumors, innuendos and hints of scandal made no difference to him. It was *her* he was worried about.

"Really, I'm fine with this," Mirabella assured him. "I appreciate you being so kind and doing this for me," she added with feeling.

"You don't want your grandmother there?" That somehow didn't sound right to him, not since she professed to care so much about the woman.

"No," Mirabella answered firmly, even though it secretly hurt her heart to keep her grandmother from attending the ceremony. "She'd want it to be more... wedding-like," Mirabella explained after a beat. "This might be a little too assembly-line for her taste. This way, I can embellish on it when I tell her about how you just whisked me off. I can make it more appealing for her. The main thing my grandmother wants is for this baby to have its father's last name and this Vegas wedding will accomplish that for her."

"All right, then," Zane agreed. "It's settled. Wednesday morning we'll fly out to Vegas and make it official."

She surprised him again by saying, "You really don't have to do this, Zane."

"Changing your mind again?" he asked, wondering what was wrong this time.

"No, I'm not. It's just that—"

He heard her hesitating and he put his own meaning to it. "Don't worry, Belle, I don't expect anything to change between us. You'll have to move in for appearances' sake, but that's as far as the cohabitating will go," he assured her. "You'll have your own room." When she still didn't say anything, he said, "Think of it like a dorm, except there'll only be two inhabitants in the whole building."

She had to stop looking for ulterior motives and hidden agendas and just graciously accept his help. "I don't know how to thank you."

"Don't worry about it. But I'll still expect you to come in tomorrow," he added, teasing her.

"I never thought differently."

The thing of it was, he thought as he replaced the landline receiver into the cradle several minutes later, he knew she didn't have to come in tomorrow—which placed her in a class all by herself.

He'd had his share of women who, even after only a short time into the relationship, expected things of him. A great many things. They took things for granted as their due. Mirabella did none of that. Even though she was supposedly going to be his wife in the eyes of the world, she didn't assume that gave her any extra privileges, any more rights than she already had.

He could do worse than to build a life with a woman like that.

And it certainly didn't hurt that he was attracted to her.

Although, he reconsidered, that might make things rather difficult in the immediate near future. They were going to be married and yet any benefits which came from a union like that were going to have to be held at arm's length. He'd given her his word it was going to be a celibate union and he wasn't the type to force himself on a woman.

He had a feeling he could easily charm Mirabella. Charm her so he could get her to want to be in his bed, but that wouldn't be the right thing to do. It certainly wouldn't be the honorable way to go. There would be no satisfaction in knowing he had to in essence seduce Mirabella in order to see just how much of the chemistry he felt between them actually existed, and how much of it was just in his head.

There was a definite lure to forbidden fruit and right now, she was that.

This, he couldn't help thinking as he went upstairs to his bedroom suite, was getting very complicated.

It wouldn't be if she weren't attractive and intriguing, and if he wasn't drawn to her, as well, Zane thought.

Would you have been so willing to step up and help her out this way if Belle had a face that could stop a clock? Zane asked himself.

In all honesty, he didn't have an answer to that question. He supposed he was just lucky no one would be asking it.

And that Mirabella looked the way she did. No one was going to question he was marrying her because they were a love match.

If they only knew, he couldn't help thinking.

Chapter 13

By the time Zane arrived at her ground floor apartment to pick her up for the airport on Wednesday morning, Mirabella felt as if her butterflies were giving birth to butterflies—and all of them were vying for space with her baby who had taken up residence there three months before them.

She left behind a bedroom in chaos. Every article of clothing she owned was no longer in the closet, but on her bed, a casualty of her search for something becoming to wear to the wedding with no guests.

"You're doing the right thing, you're doing the right thing," she kept telling herself over and over again, chanting the sentence as if it was some sort of magical mantra that would, perforce, become true through sheer repetition.

Butterflies now on full alert, she closed the door

behind her and was halfway down the walk before she suddenly doubled back. She'd forgotten to lock her apartment door.

"Sorry," she apologized, hurrying to Zane's dark sedan and getting into the passenger seat. "I didn't want to leave the apartment unlocked."

"No reason to apologize. It's not as if the plane's going to leave without us, seeing as how we're the only passengers. Did you remember to bring a valid ID?"

He'd reminded her of that yesterday, just before they left the office for the evening. He had a friend pull strings at the Clark County Clerk's Office in Nevada, assuring him the marriage license would be waiting for them when they arrived. All that was needed was proof of ID on both their parts.

"I've got my driver's license in my purse," she told him.

"Good." He glanced over to make sure Mirabella had buckled up before he started the vehicle again. "You're wearing that?" he asked as he drove out of the complex.

Mirabella looked down at the two-piece suit she'd finally decided on. Light blue, it was the most expensive outfit she owned and she rarely wore it, trying to keep it new looking.

"Yes. Why? What's wrong with it?" she asked, her confidence, what little there was of it this morning, swiftly ebbing away.

"Nothing," he said, "if you're going to a meeting. But this is supposed to be your wedding. I would have thought you'd be wearing something a little more—" he wasn't good at descriptions, he just knew what he liked when he saw it "—well, festively elegant."

Zane was undoubtedly accustomed to the women who moved around in high society circles, she thought, trying to ignore the sting to her pride. He probably had no idea what it was like to have to budget money from month to month, to save up for something rather than just purchase it because he had a whim.

"Sorry," she replied. "This is the best I've got."

"It's okay, we can remedy that," Zane told her. "And stop apologizing so much. You can't just keep assuming you're always in the wrong. You're entitled to your own opinions, your own tastes—and your own mistakes," he added, glancing back at her suit.

He obviously viewed what she had on as one of those "mistakes" she was entitled to. "What do you mean, 'we can remedy that'?" she wanted to know, doing her best not to take offense. Exactly what did he have in mind for a so-called remedy?

He was catching all the green lights for once. The private airfield wasn't far now.

"Once we land in Vegas," he told her, "I'll take you shopping." He'd made arrangements for a car to be waiting for him. "There're some exclusive boutiques along Via Bellagio—and a few of them actually have some rather nice clothes," he teased with an amused smile. "A high price tag does not always ensure a decent-looking outfit," he pointed out.

There was no way she could go on the shopping trip he was talking about. "I didn't bring my credit cards," Mirabella confessed as they got out of his sedan and walked to the corporate jet.

"Don't worry about it." Zane could see she was about to protest, most likely stressing she *was* worried about it. Her grandmother was right, he couldn't help thinking. In her own mild, unassuming way, this was one very stubborn woman. "Consider it my wedding present to you."

Holding on to the handrail, Mirabella made her way up the steps to the jet.

A flight attendant stood in the open cabin door, a welcoming smile on her lips.

"But this isn't a *real* wedding," Mirabella reminded him.

Zane pretended to review the key ingredients that were going into this undertaking. "Wedding license, chapel, licensed minister officiating, it's real, all right," he assured her, walking into the plane directly behind her.

He pointed out available seats in the body of the jet plane. Other than the captain and the attendant, they were the only two people on the flight.

"I think the term you're looking for is *marriage of convenience*," Zane prompted. "Marriages of convenience," he went on, "are still real in the eyes of the law. They're just struck up for different reasons. Given some of the reasons people have for getting married— money, connections, using deception for their own selfish reasons—this marriage doesn't rank that poorly."

Selecting a seat, Zane sat down, then gestured to the seat next to him. "Sit," he urged. "Relax. Everything's going to be fine."

She wished she could believe that, but even with Zane's easygoing assurances, her pulse refused to settle down and stop racing.

True to his word, before they ever entered the chapel where they were to exchange their vows—or rather, repeat the words fed to them by some inattentive minister who chose speed over quality and made his money by the ceremony, not by the hour, which was how Mirabella envisioned the whole wedding—Zane took her shopping.

She had only seen places like the shops he took her to and the clothes displayed there on the pages of magazines she'd occasionally thumbed through at the checkout counter. She didn't even bother buying those magazines because she knew the clothes they featured belonged in a world she would never inhabit. What was the point of wistfully looking, then?

And yet, here she was, looking at those clothes as Zane selectively went through the racks, reviewing what was being offered.

The clothes whizzed by so quickly on their hangers, she hardly had a chance to look at them.

But then, she had a feeling her opinion really didn't matter here. After all, she'd picked out something to wear to the wedding he had already indicated didn't come anywhere close to making the grade.

Her opinion was just to wait and see, she thought, not to render any opinions no matter what he had said to the contrary previously.

"How about this one?" Zane asked after spending several minutes engaged in swift perusal, going through the dresses in the shop like a dealer going through a deck of cards.

Turning to face her, Zane held a white lace dress up against her. The hem was an inch shy of brushing along her knees. Fitted to the waist, with three-quarter-length sleeves and an A-line skirt, the material felt as if it had been spun out of a cloud.

"It's stunning," Mirabella whispered. She'd never owned anything so beautiful in her life.

"No, a dress's job is to make the wearer look stunning," he corrected. And then, as if appraising the wedding dress's effect, he nodded. "It passes the test. We'll take it," he announced to the saleswoman who was doing her best not to hover too closely.

As the woman approached, Zane told her, "We'll need shoes and some sort of hair accessory to match." He turned to Mirabella. "Unless you'd rather wear a veil instead?"

"No, a hair accessory will be fine," she assured him. She was fine with anything he picked out for her. And then her eyes widened as she saw the price tag affixed to the dress he had selected for her. "Is that for the dress, or the whole store?" she asked, amazed anyone could charge that much for a dress without holding a gun in their hand.

He laughed. "It's a Vera Wang," he pointed out. "It's for the dress."

"Would the young lady like to try it on?" the saleswoman wanted to know. They both looked at Mirabella for an answer.

"It's my size, it'll fit," she said. She'd *make* it fit, she added silently. "Besides, it's bad luck for the groom to see the bride in the wedding dress before the wedding."

The words had just come tumbling out. The moment they did, she felt like a complete idiot. Those superstitions were for people who were actually getting married, not going through the motions of a charade, the way they were.

"The young lady is absolutely right," the saleswoman agreed with a smile.

Mirabella had a feeling that, given what Zane was spending at the store, the saleswoman would have agreed if he'd speculated the old adage about the moon being made of green cheese was actually true.

"I'll pay you back for these," Mirabella told him as they walked out of the boutique. "It might take me a year or two," she added honestly, thinking of what all the items had come to, "but I'll pay you back."

"I already told you, Belle, consider it a wedding present. And don't start arguing with me on our wedding day," he cautioned as she opened her mouth to do just that. "That is definitely considered bad luck."

"I never heard of that one," Mirabella said as she went around to the passenger side.

Loading the bags from the boutique into the truck, he closed the lid and walked back to the driver's side of the vehicle. "That's because I just made it up."

Mirabella laughed softly in response. He found himself liking the sound of her laugh more and more.

"Next stop, County Clerk's Office," he announced as he pulled away from the curb. "I could rent a room at the hotel," he offered. "That way you could change into your wedding dress there instead of in the chapel."

"No, that's all right, you've already gone to a great deal of expense. The chapel's got to have somewhere I can change."

"What if it doesn't?" he challenged.

"It's got to have a restroom," she reasoned. "I can change there. I don't need much."

"Apparently not," he agreed.

Since he had everything prepared ahead of time, picking up the license turned out to be a matter of producing their photo IDs and signing the license in the proper spaces, then paying the posted fee. From start to finish, the entire process took a little longer than ordering a meal to-go in a fast-food restaurant.

Vegas was known for speed in these matters.

The last part of their Vegas adventure entailed finding a chapel.

There were, she quickly discovered, a myriad to choose from. There appeared to be something for everyone's taste, be it color—blue was popular, but there were others in red, lime, rainbow, etcetera—or theme—Elvis still held sway, but there were chapels featuring Western scenarios and others that appealed to people who had always loved traveling circuses.

Zane drove by all of them, making her think that perhaps he was the one having second thoughts now.

Gathering her courage, she said, "Look, it's okay if you changed your mind—"

He spared her a quick glance. Traffic was beginning to pick up. "Why would you think I changed my mind?" he asked, passing a chapel called 'til Death Do Us Part—If Not Sooner.

"You've driven by a number of chapels already—a lot of chapels, actually—and you haven't stopped, so I just thought maybe you'd changed your mind about all this—and that's okay," she quickly qualified. "I understand—"

"No, you don't," he contradicted. "I drove by all the other chapels because I was driving to this one."

When she looked, she realized they had arrived at a rather small chapel that appeared to be modeled after a quaint little country church.

"How do you like this one?" Zane asked her, slowing the car so she could get a better look.

"It's lovely," she told him, surprised and touched he'd gone to the trouble of finding a chapel that actually *looked* the part. From what she had heard from others, one chapel was just as good as another for their purposes.

"Yes, I thought you might like this," he said, driving to the rear of the small chapel. Behind it was a tiny cottage, just to the side of the limited parking lot. "The cottage belongs to the chapel. The minister, Reverend Applegate, and his wife live in it," he told her. "I'm sure if we asked Mrs. Applegate, she'd have no objections to you changing into your wedding dress there."

Just as he pulled his car into a parking spot, the reverend's wife, a motherly looking woman in her sixties, came out of the cottage.

Shading her eyes from the sun, she squinted a little as she looked in his direction. "Mr. Colton?" Mrs. Applegate asked.

"She knows you?" Mirabella turned from the woman to look at him quizzically.

"I called ahead." He could feel Mirabella's eyes on him, questions multiplying in her mind. "I try not to leave too many things to chance."

That made sense—and she liked that explanation a lot better than what she was thinking. "Oh, I figured maybe you'd been married here before."

He laughed out loud at the idea. With all he'd had to deal with over the years, he'd never even given any serious thought to marriage, much less gone through with one.

"No, this is my first marriage," he replied.

But not your last, Mirabella couldn't help thinking. She knew she should be grateful he was going through all this trouble for her and her unborn child, but there was a part of her—granted, a selfish part, she admitted ruefully—that wished all of this was for real and for keeps, instead of just for show and only temporary.

"You're early," Mrs. Applegate told Zane. "The reverend's in the chapel, getting prepared for the ceremony." Then, turning to Mirabella, she said, "Let's get you ready, my dear. Your bouquet arrived a little while ago. Your young man has excellent taste," she confided, then added, "And you are going to make a beautiful bride."

Taking the shopping bags from her, Mrs. Applegate led Mirabella to the cottage.

"We'll be back soon," the older woman promised Zane just before she walked into the house.

She couldn't take her eyes off herself.

She hadn't thought she could look this beautiful, this breathtakingly stunning.

It's the dress, not you, she chided herself. *Now let's go, before Zane comes to his senses and changes his mind.*

"There," Mrs. Applegate declared, stepping back and admiring her part in getting Mirabella ready. She paused for a second, giving the pearl hair clip a final minor adjustment. "You look like a vision, my dear." Picking up the bouquet she had on the side table, Mrs. Applegate thrust it into Mirabella's hands. "Now, let's get you married."

"Let's," Mirabella whispered. It was meant to come out like a positive statement, but at the last moment, her voice had faltered.

Strains of the wedding march began to fill the little chapel the moment she stepped over the threshold.

Zane, standing at the altar, turned expectantly in her direction. He wasn't prepared to see her looking like this and for a moment or two, he couldn't do anything but simply stare at her as if he was some pubescent teenager.

Mirabella looked even more beautiful than he'd anticipated.

Mirabella didn't remember walking down the short aisle, didn't remember clutching the bouquet so hard, she all but severed the flower stems. One moment, she was crossing the chapel threshold, the next she was standing beside Zane with no clear recollection of how she got there.

It was a little similar to the way she felt about how she had gotten to this place in her life, standing in a tiny chapel in Las Vegas, three months pregnant and marrying a man who hadn't gotten her that way.

Mrs. Applegate discreetly stepped forward to take the bouquet from her so her hand was free to be joined to Zane's.

Reverend Applegate looked like the photograph her grandmother had of her own father on her wedding day, Mirabella thought, instantly warming to the man, just as she had to his wife. They both had a kindly appearance and were not at all what she would have expected to find in a city that performed wholesale weddings. It was as if the Applegates had been born to be the people they now were, a minister and his wife.

Reverend Applegate began to speak.

This might, in reality, be just a sham marriage, but Mirabella still listened intently as the minister said the words that, in the eyes of the world, would bind her to Zane.

At least for now.

There was no one else in the chapel except for the four of them. Even so, Reverend Applegate said, "If anyone has any objections why this man and this woman should not be joined in holy matrimony, speak now or forever hold your piece."

Mirabella realized she was holding her breath, half expecting someone to pop up out of nowhere and speak up.

But no one did.

The rest of the ceremony proceeded without any interruption or incident. And then, before she could fully absorb it, Reverend Applegate pronounced them "husband and wife."

Her heart raced even harder.

"You may now kiss the bride," Reverend Applegate told Zane.

She expected Zane to kiss her on the cheek. At the very most, she expected him to give her a peck on the lips. She didn't expect him to take her into his arms and actually press his lips to hers.

And she definitely didn't expect him to completely rock her world.

Chapter 14

It wasn't as if she'd never been kissed before. She had. She had even half fancied herself in love once before. That had been back in college when everyone she knew had seemed to be pairing off and she desperately wanted to be part of what was going on rather than just left sitting on the sidelines.

But despite her best efforts to emulate her friends, she came to realize it was more like she was trying to talk herself into being in love rather than actually feeling any of the exhilarating side effects that came from experiencing love. The first and foremost of these side effects would have been to be on the receiving end of a kiss that threatened to eclipse the sun, the moon and all the stars.

She truthfully had never even come close to feeling something like that.

Until just now.

Suddenly, all the things she'd once believed were really only fabrications of some romance storyteller's overactive imagination—the racing heart, the swirling room, the darkening surroundings, all of that—she realized were most assuredly absolutely true.

And she knew this because *her* heart was racing, the room she was in was whirling around her like a sped up merry-go-round, and now everything was beginning to shrink down to less than a pinpoint before it all suddenly went to black.

Leaving nothing behind except for the man who was kissing her and the kiss itself, the kiss that was causing this huge detonation to go off inside her.

Was this *really* happening?

One moment, she was going through what she'd convinced herself to view as a necessary charade, the next moment every molecule that went into the making up her body had astoundingly come to life.

And was eagerly wanting more.

People sucked into the eye of a hurricane undoubtedly experienced a more stable environment than she was experiencing right at this second. Her breath, as well as her orientation, was almost completely gone. All she could do to keep from being blown away was to hold on to Zane for dear life.

That, and kiss back.

It was one hell of a surprise. Zane hadn't expected to have his world shaken up like this. The best way he could think to describe it was likening it to crossing a solid piece of terrain and suddenly discovering there was no ground beneath his feet at all.

It wasn't even like trying to walk across quicksand because in that case there was at least *something* there that made him think he could attempt to cross it. But the ground he believed was there had just vanished entirely and he now found himself experiencing the sensation of free-falling through space.

It was exhilarating and frightening at the same time.

The sweetness that surprised him was indescribable.

Her lips tasted of some sort of sweet flavor he couldn't begin to place. All he knew was he liked it—and he wanted more.

His arms tightened around her as he tried, to the best of his ability, to make sense of it all, to make sense of the intense reaction he was having to this woman.

But he failed, just as he suspected he might.

It didn't make sense.

What it did do was make him uneasy because feeling the way he suddenly did, he realized keeping Mirabella at arm's length was going to be very, very difficult. After all, he had told her—all but given his word—nothing would change between them privately. Even though they were now legally married, he'd promised not to take advantage of that—or of her.

Attracted to her though he was when he'd said it, Zane had thought keeping his distance would be easy enough to do, he would just exercise his self-control. But what he hadn't bargained for was being *this* drawn to her.

This was, he couldn't help thinking, going to be one hell of a challenge.

A very distant noise vaguely caught his attention. When it came again, louder this time, it managed to undulate into his consciousness. That was when Zane realized Reverend Applegate was clearing his throat in an attempt to get their attention and terminate the kiss he had instructed them to initiate before the day grew old.

"Now then," Reverend Applegate told them with a chuckle, "go out and start your new lives—and try to wait until you at least get back to your hotel room," he added with a knowing wink.

Zane paused to shake the minister's hand, pressing an additional hundred dollar bill into it. "Thanks for fitting us in so quickly, Reverend, instead of making us wait," he told the older man.

The smile on the minister's lips was genuine. "My pleasure, Mr. Colton. Nice to see a calm, clear-headed couple exchanging vows for a change instead of two people propping one another up because they're both utterly inebriated and suddenly decided, in the middle of that dense alcoholic haze, it was a good idea to get married." Reverend Applegate beamed at them. "Have a good life together," he said, meaning every word.

"Wait," Mrs. Applegate cautioned to keep them from leaving the chapel just then. "Now look this way and smile!"

Before Mirabella had a chance to process the woman's words, the minister's wife had snapped the camera she was holding in her hands three times in succession. "One of these should turn out," she assured them. "If you give me your email address, I can send them to you." Mrs. Applegate's words were addressed to her.

Still feeling somewhat dazed, Mirabella gave her the information she'd requested.

"Perfect," Mrs. Applegate declared, jotting it down.

"You'll have them within the hour. Come, I'll walk you out," she offered, then added on an explanatory note, "There's another couple waiting for the reverend."

"Of course," Zane said amicably, ushering Mirabella out behind Mrs. Applegate.

Leading the way out of the chapel, the minister's wife brought them to the front door. "Be good to one another," she advised. "And never go to bed angry. It's worked for the reverend and me for the last forty years," she confided with a wink. "Remember, words of love are so much better to say—and hear—than words of anger."

"Thank you for everything," Mirabella said to the older woman.

The latter waved the words of thanks away. "I didn't do anything. It was the reverend who did all the work."

Hugging them each one at a time, Mrs. Applegate then turned her attention to the couple waiting in the wings.

"Guess I'd better change out of this and into my clothes again," Mirabella said, looking down at her wedding dress. She ran her hands lovingly over the bridal dress's skirt. "I left them in the cottage," she told Zane needlessly.

"Do you want me to wait in the car?" he asked her, sensing Mirabella needed a little time to herself to process everything.

Her first inclination was to answer yes, she wanted him in the car because she needed distance between them in order to regroup. But then she remembered the minister's wife had to help her with the dress's zipper. Getting the zipper down would most likely present the same problem as pulling it up had.

"I think I'm going to need you to get me started." The second the words were out, Mirabella realized how it had to have sounded to him and color instantly materialized—a bright, bright pink—and climbed up to her cheeks. She tried to go into damage control mode. "I mean the zipper, it's—"

"I understand what you mean," he said, doing his best not to look amused over how flustered she was. Once again it occurred to him there was something incredibly vulnerable about her and he found himself having the same reaction he'd had before—he wanted to protect her.

Entering the cottage behind her, he asked, "Where did you leave your clothes?"

"This way." She led the way down the small hallway and then entered a room off to the right. Her suit was on the bed where Mrs. Applegate had laid it out for her. "I just need you to move the zipper down to the middle of my back."

She didn't trust him, he thought. Otherwise, her directions wouldn't be so specific. She'd just tell him to pull down the zipper.

"Sure thing," he told her.

Mirabella turned her back to him and waited, unconsciously holding her breath. When she felt Zane slide the zipper slowly down from her neck, she could feel her pulse beginning to quicken—just the way it had when he had taken her into his arms in the chapel.

Maybe it was her imagination, but it seemed to her that Zane was moving the zipper down almost in slow motion and with every fraction of a second that passed by, she could feel herself growing more aroused. Could feel herself struggling not to turn around and discover whether a second kiss held the same thrill for her as the first one had.

Get a grip, Mirabella. Don't get needy. And for heaven's sake, don't mess up.

Taking a breath, Mirabella forced herself to continue to face the wall as she said, "Thank you. I can take it from here."

Was it her imagination, or had her voice quavered just then?

"I'll be in the car," Zane murmured, walking out of the room.

He doubted Mirabella would ever know just how much self-control he was exercising right at this moment by walking away. Because it took all that control not to turn her around and draw her back into his arms while he slid the dress from her shoulders and let it fall to the floor.

It hit him with the speed and force of a lightning bolt.

He realized he really wanted to make love with her. Make love with the woman that Clark County had legally made his wife.

The irony of it did not fail to register.

He walked hurriedly out of the house without turning around.

Mirabella quickly stepped out of her wedding dress. Then, before putting her suit back on, she paused to pick up the dress and fold it. She spared herself a moment longer just to run her fingertips lovingly over the material.

Married. I'm married. I'm Mrs. Zane Colton. Who would have ever thought...?

She spared herself one more moment, then quickly

put on her skirt and jacket. She didn't want to keep Zane waiting. Certainly not after he had put himself out like this for her.

Rather than wait in the car the way he had told her he would, Zane waited right outside the cottage door. He snapped to attention the second he saw her come out.

"We'd better get going," Zane said, taking Mirabella's arm as he walked her over to where he'd parked the rented vehicle.

Feeling as if her feet weren't touching the ground, Mirabella fell into step beside the man who was, for all intents and purposes, her brand-new husband.

He made the offer one final time in case she had changed her mind. "You know, if you want, we can stay in Vegas for the night. I'm sure for the right price—" which by his tone of voice he indicated he was more than willing to offer—money had long since ceased being a problem for his family "—a honeymoon suite could become available." Zane waited for her response.

Mirabella pressed her lips together. She could still taste him. With any luck, that wouldn't fade for a couple of hours, she hoped, a shiver hopscotching along her spine.

Don't get carried away. So he kissed you. There was an audience watching, remember? What did you expect him to do when the reverend said to kiss the bride, punt you over the goal post? Of course he kissed you, but it didn't mean anything to him. Remember that.

"No, we'd better just fly back. You have all those

meetings scheduled in the morning," she reminded him, the words tasting like tree bark in her mouth. "It's best to prepare for them today."

Zane laughed softly, shaking his head. Any other woman would have jumped to take him up on his suggestion without a single thought to anything else. "Always watching out for me, aren't you, Belle?"

"That's what you pay me to do, isn't it?" she asked him.

"It is, indeed," Zane agreed, but he didn't really sound very happy as he said it.

She wondered if she'd offended him somehow, or if he was suddenly having second thoughts.

She couldn't really blame him if he was, she thought as she fell silent.

"I can have someone sent over to your place to pack up your things in the morning," Zane casually mentioned once they were on the jet again.

When Mirabella looked at him quizzically, he realized she'd probably forgotten their earlier conversation regarding logistics after the wedding.

"Remember, I said we were going to have to live together for appearances' sake and my house is probably quite a bit bigger than yours."

So she had heard, Mirabella thought. "You don't have to send anyone. I can pack up my things. There isn't all that much to pack, really," she confessed.

He shook his head. "Turning down help with menial work. You have got to be the most unassuming woman I've ever met, Belle."

She offered him a half smile.

He looked beneath the surface. She was upset, he

suspected. Why? He thought this was what she wanted. Obviously, he'd overlooked something.

"What's wrong?" he asked her.

"I just hate the idea of giving up my apartment. It's in a really nice location. I doubt I'll be able to find something like it once this is finally over." She flushed as the words replayed themselves in her head. "I'm sorry, that didn't come out right—"

He waved her apology aside. He had no need to hear any apologies. "If that's all that's bothering you, don't worry about it. I'll take care of the lease," he promised. "You can still go over to your apartment whenever you want.

"Leave your furniture there, too," he recommended. "God knows we've got enough of that at the house. Just bring whatever you don't want to leave behind. Clothes, mementos, things like that," he told her. "The rest can stay in your apartment."

"You don't mind me keeping my apartment?" she asked, surprised.

"I said I'd pay for it, didn't I? So why should I mind?" He didn't understand her reasoning. "Even if this was actually a marriage, I don't have the right to change you any more than you would have the right to change me. When two people enter a marriage these days, it's not as a master and his servant, but as two equals."

The plane encountered a little turbulence. He saw her digging her nails into the armrests. "I just thought since you were doing this favor for me," she explained, "that well, I owed you."

"Maybe I'll ask you for your firstborn when this is over." The horrified look that passed over her face made him realize she thought he might be serious. "I'm just kidding," he assured her, running his hand along her arm to comfort her.

"I knew that," she murmured.

She looked down at the wedding ring on her finger. The diamonds along the band were gleaming brightly enough to blind someone. "What do you want me to do with this?"

He pretended to regard her question for a moment. "Right off the top of my head, I'd say wear it."

She regarded it uneasily. "But the ring's real, right?"

"It is." Zane nodded, adding, "Unless the jeweler lied to me."

She felt a tremendous responsibility just wearing the ring. "Don't you want to put this into a safe or something?"

He didn't quite see it that way. "There's no point in having something beautiful if you can't show it off," he told her.

For one very heady moment, Mirabella had the impression he wasn't really talking about the ring on her finger, but about her.

Chapter 15

"I have to admit," Zane said, breaking the prolonged silence in his sedan later that evening as he drove into Mirabella's garden apartment complex, "when I thought about finally getting married, this was not exactly the way I envisioned my wedding night going—dropping off my wife at her apartment and then driving home." He spared her a glance. She'd been almost stoically quiet during the short trip from the office. "I imagine it's the same for you."

There was kindness in his voice rather than the usual professional distance she had come to expect because of their work relationship. But then, none of this was exactly in the parameters of a professional relationship, now was it? Mirabella thought.

Quite honestly, she really didn't know *what* it was, what *any* of what had happened today was—other than really, really confusing.

"No, I guess not," she finally responded in a voice barely louder than a whisper.

Mirabella was experiencing ambivalent feelings about every aspect of today. At times, such as now, ambivalence was trumped by guilt. She knew she was in Zane's debt and it wasn't a place she wanted to be because she had no way of repaying him, nothing to trade in return for what Zane was doing for her.

"And you didn't have to go through the trouble of bringing me home," she told him as he headed for one of the complex's guest parking strips. "I mean, you have things to do…"

"Sure I did," he contradicted her. "I picked you up this morning, remember? That meant you had no way of getting back to your apartment. Someone had to drive you here and who better than your husband?" he asked her with a hint of a smile.

A smile Mirabella couldn't quite read.

"Husband in name only," she reminded Zane, trying to make him understand, despite the supposed new roles they'd assumed, she expected nothing from him—not even a ride home. That he'd already done far more than she'd ever thought possible.

Zane inclined his head in tacit agreement. "But nonetheless, your husband. This isn't putting me out, Belle," he assured her, "if that's what you're thinking. I like driving."

Because she didn't know what else to do, Mirabella nodded as he brought the car to a stop in one of the available guest parking spaces. This unexpected turn in her life was so new, she had no idea what to say or how to feel, other than grateful, which she was.

But she was also very confused about her feelings,

not the least of which was this immensely strong attraction she was doing her damnedest to block. Looking back, she would have had to admit she'd always been attracted to him. But after that kiss at the altar, everything had gotten shaken up as far as she was concerned. All she could do was think about Zane. Think about the man in ways that had absolutely nothing even remotely to do with work.

She had the night to get all of it under control, Mirabella told herself. She intended to do just that.

Opening the door on her side, she was about to get out, but Zane proved to be much faster than she was. He had rounded the trunk and was there on her side of the car to help her out by the time she set one foot on the paved ground.

Taking her hand, he brought her out of the sedan. "Are you sure I can't take you out to dinner?" he offered again.

The truth was, he was feeling oddly guilty about this whole setup. To his way of thinking, she'd been shortchanged all around, a victim of mindless gossip as well as some man's disrespect which had left her alone and pregnant. He still just couldn't understand how a person could have walked away from someone who looked like Mirabella, moreover, someone who had all of her resolute, kind qualities.

"It doesn't seem right, just getting married, then bringing you back to the office and now leaving you on your doorstep without doing *something* by way of acknowledging and celebrating the occasion," Zane insisted.

"You *have* done a great deal," Mirabella countered. Then, as she took her key out of her purse, she paused. He was right, this *did* feel strange, just parting abruptly like this. The man had flown her out to Vegas, bought her a wedding dress and then married her. Maybe Zane wanted to talk, she thought.

Looking at him over her shoulder, she asked, "Would you like to come in for some coffee?"

It was on the tip of his tongue to politely turn her down. He didn't want her to feel that she had to ask him in. A lot had happened today and there was a lot to process—for both of them. But he didn't want to just abandon her if she was asking him in. And, he supposed he should try to act sociable. After all, they were going to be in a social situation the second news of this so-called marriage became public knowledge. He needed to be able to behave comfortably in her company, otherwise, questions would crop up—undoubtedly starting with his own family, Zane realized.

"Sure," he acquiesced. "Why not?"

Crossing the threshold, Mirabella immediately turned on the light. The second the light illuminated her apartment, she was struck by how very surreal all of this really was. This morning, when she'd left her apartment, she'd been a single woman. A *pregnant* single woman, but a single woman nonetheless. She'd returned to her apartment a married one.

Granted the marriage was, for all intents and purposes, in name only, but as far as everyone outside of just the two of them was concerned, she was a married woman.

As far back as she could remember, she had never felt as unsure of herself as she did right at this very moment. Turning to close the door, her purse slipped from her fingers. Zane moved to retrieve the purse at the same time as she did and they wound up bumping heads.

Regaining her balance, Mirabella rubbed the top of her head. "Sorry," she quickly apologized.

Zane handed the purse to her. "For dropping your purse or bumping my head?"

She deposited her purse on the kitchen counter several steps away from the front door. "Both."

"Well, stop it," he told her. When she looked at him uncertainly, he tried to make her see what he meant. "You've got to police yourself and stop apologizing for everything. Everything is not your fault, Belle. And even if it was, you're a Colton now." He pointed out the obvious—and something that had been drummed into his own head by his mother. "Coltons don't apologize."

"You do," Mirabella recalled. "I've heard you apologize."

Maybe he had, once or twice, but definitely not with the frequency she seemed to. "Not constantly," he emphasized.

She lowered her head, doing her best to suppress a sigh. Zane was right. As usual.

"Point taken."

Surprising her, Zane placed his hands on her shoulders, momentarily holding her in place. Then, with one hand still on her shoulder, he raised her chin with his other hand, bringing her eyes level with his.

"Not yet, I don't think," he appraised, searching her eyes. "But work on it."

"Yes, sir—um, Mr. Col—Zane," Mirabella finally said after two self-corrections.

"Zane. It's Zane," he reminded her. His eyes crinkled then. "Not exactly an auspicious start for a married couple, is it?" he asked with a laugh.

A self-deprecating smile played on her lips. "No, it's not," she agreed.

"Say that with conviction," he coached.

"No, it's not," Mirabella repeated, deepening her voice to give the words some weight.

"Still not there," he told her. "Say it like I'm a cat burglar breaking in to your apartment and the only way you're going to get me to jump back out the window is to say that first word with enough force to literally *push* me back."

This time, tired of coming up lacking, Mirabella shouted the word into his face. *"No!"*

Success, Zane thought with a touch of triumph. "Atta girl!" he laughed, pulling her into his arms to give her a hug. He'd begun to think maybe she wasn't nearly as feisty as he'd initially thought she was.

Zane quickly discovered the problem with a spontaneous hug was that in order for the hug to be genuine and effective, it had to bring two people into exceedingly close proximity. Putting them practically into each other's breast pockets.

Moreover, he found that closeness brought with it a whole myriad of other feelings, some of which were supposed to be kept tightly under wraps.

Hugging negated that unspoken arrangement.

The scent of her perfume, something Zane now realized he'd been aware of on a subconscious level for quite a while, seemed to seductively fill his head. It almost perversely stirred things within him that were better off left undisturbed.

Awareness of the danger came too late.

The sciences had never held any allure for him in school, but even he knew it had been scientifically proven that once rung, bells could not be unrung. And so it was that dormant emotions, once stirred, could not be effectively unstirred.

And definitely not immediately.

The laughter that had been on his lips faded as other, more urgent reactions rose to the surface, reminding him that because of this matter with his stepfather and so many other pressing things that had gotten in the way, he hadn't had the time to just step back and *feel*. Hadn't taken the time to just step back and be a regular, flesh-and-blood man who had simple, ordinary needs.

And this woman who was currently in his arms, who because of extenuating circumstances he had made his wife, both ignited those needs and could help to quell and satiate those very same needs.

Before he could think it through, and certainly before he could stop himself, Zane lowered his mouth to hers and kissed Mirabella.

Kissed her because the first time had been so good.

Kissed her because he wanted to revisit that first time and continue on from there.

In her heart, Mirabella had to admit she knew the moment she'd suggested Zane come in, it would lead to this. But what astonished her was her customary hesitation, her uncertainty, her reticence, none of it was present as she found herself on the receiving end of Zane's passionate kiss.

She *wanted* this.

A second before his lips touched hers, she found

herself anxiously *waiting* for this. If he hadn't kissed her, she would have very possibly taken matters into her own hands and kissed *him*.

Yes, she had kept reinforcing the fact that all this was in name only, but it was really to reassure him, not herself. She didn't want Zane thinking because he'd extended a kindness to her by giving her baby an established last name and hopefully silencing whoever was out there sending those vicious emails, that she wanted something more from him. That she *expected* something more from him. That all this was a plan on her part and she was a gold digger, or even worse.

She desperately didn't want Zane thinking she was trying to trap him in any manner, shape or form.

But she did want him to know she was grateful to him. And therefore, no strings were attached to—or resulting from—what was happening here.

This was just a matter of two consenting adults—consenting.

And right now, Mirabella thought as desire shivered all through her, what she was consenting to was pure ecstasy.

Her breathing grew more erratic with each passing moment and her body felt as if it was going to ignite right on the spot.

She couldn't wait.

Somewhere in the back of his mind, on some level, Zane knew he should stop right now.

But he couldn't.

Mirabella wasn't his prisoner, which was what he was afraid she'd think. If anyone was anyone's prisoner here, he was hers. He couldn't just stop and walk away from her now if his very life depended on it. The only thing that could possibly get him to do that was if he felt *she* wanted him to stop.

But each time he tried to draw his head back in order to catch his breath and give her the option of calling a halt to this, Mirabella would frame his face between her hands and urgently press her lips to his.

Keeping the connection from breaking.

Feeding the anticipation.

His head was spinning and all he could think about was making love with her.

Having her.

Losing himself in her.

His lips never leaving hers, Zane began peeling off her clothing—she was back in that sensible suit she'd had on when he first came to pick her up this morning.

With each article he teased off her body, Zane could feel himself getting more and more excited. Could feel his body literally *aching* for her.

She intoxicated him as anticipation drummed through his veins. Zane reverently slid his hands along her body, absorbing every nuance, every curve. Awed by the way she gave herself to him at the same time that she imprisoned him.

Awed as well by the fact that he had worked alongside this woman for four years without ever really suspecting how deep her still waters really ran.

Mirabella was amazed at the feelings racing through her, amazed at the way she responded to Zane. She might have been pregnant, but she was far from experienced. The realization hit her hard because here, with this man, she was feeling things she'd never felt before, doing things she'd never done.

Wanting to do things she'd never done before.

It was almost as if her body had taken over and she was just going along for the ride, hanging on for dear life and loving every second of it.

The moment Zane had begun undressing her, she had started to do the same with him.

It was jacket for jacket, his slacks for her skirt, his shirt for hers. The same one-for-one policy applied to underwear.

Her heart was racing and pounding more and more as each piece was separated from its owner and fell to the floor.

And then it was just them. No clothing, no barriers, nothing but raw emotions demanding to be heeded, to be appeased and thrilled.

It felt as if every fiber of her body had come not just awake but supremely alive.

She'd never felt like this before, capable of doing everything and anything. And all the while, she felt something building up within her, something moving ever upward toward the distant pinnacle that loomed far above her.

Her body was perspiring, pulsating with anticipation of she had no idea what. She'd never been down this path before, never felt her body quickening to this degree before.

With his lips once again sealed to hers, Zane created the union they were both more than ready for.

The second he entered her, he felt her arch against him, saw the look on her face as wonder began to trace its imprint over it.

He moved, watching her, growing more excited himself just by seeing her expression intensify.

The tempo increased until there was no turning back. One final thrust and the stars exploded over both of them. Her cry of sheer ecstasy echoed in his ears and in his head.

Chapter 16

It was the noise that woke her.

It wasn't that it was a loud noise. On the contrary, it was the kind of muffled, subdued noise someone made when they were trying very had *not* to make any noise at all.

Specifically, Mirabella realized as she opened her eyes and saw him, it was the kind of soft sounds that accompanied someone attempting to get dressed and leave without creating the slightest disturbance.

Isolated in silence, the slightest movement, the slightest deviation was amplified and thus disturbed that silence.

She had no idea what time it was, only that Zane was leaving.

"Is it time to go?" she asked. The pillow beneath her head had just the slightest hint of his scent. She gathered it to her, inhaling. Comforted by it.

Damn, he thought he was being so quiet, collecting his things together in almost slow motion in order to not accidentally hit anything, drop anything, make any sound that might cause her to wake up.

How had she managed to hear him?

Caught in the act, dressed except for his shoes and shirt, Zane sat down on the edge of her bed and slipped his shoes on. "For me, yes."

"But not for me?" she questioned, confused. They worked together, separated by only a few feet. Why didn't he want her coming into the office? Had what happened between them last night changed everything?

Zane addressed his words to the wall. Looking in her direction might have him changing his mind. "I thought you might want the day off to pack whatever you want to take with you."

He could only resist for so long. Turning his head, he caught her looking at him quizzically. Sleep was still evident in her eyes and her hair was tousled. He felt the pull of desire begin.

"To my house, remember?" he prompted.

"Oh, right." Sitting up now, Mirabella drew the sheet up with her, modestly tucking it around her. "That won't take me too long. I can be ready in fifteen, twenty minutes if you want to go in together."

"Can't," he told her, although heaven knew he was tempted. So tempted to linger with her.

But that would only make a complicated situation that much more complicated. His reasons for marrying her had been straightforward and simple. Bringing emotions into it would only muddy the waters.

But it was getting harder to hold them at bay, he realized. "I've got an early meeting with Meyer."

"About the person who set us up?" she guessed hopefully.

"Among other things," he said vaguely. "I've got to go." There was urgency infused into his tone.

He was holding her at arm's length, Mirabella thought. She had no right to ask for an accounting. "All right," she replied quietly.

She didn't believe him, Zane realized. Not that he blamed her. In her place, *he* wouldn't have believed him, either.

Last night vividly replayed itself in his mind. He should have left her alone, should have been able to resist and just gone on home.

"I'm sorry about last night," he told her.

"That bad, huh?" she quipped, trying her best not to let him see how devastated she felt by his apology and how much it hurt.

He stared at her, not comprehending her meaning for a moment.

"What?" And then the words became clear. "No, no it wasn't."

That didn't make any sense. "Then why are you sorry?" She wanted to know.

He didn't want to spell it out, but if that's what it took to make amends, he would. "Because I took advantage. Of the situation, of you."

She was looking at him as if he had lapsed into a foreign language she was desperately trying to understand. "Did you?"

"Well, yes." But he didn't want her to think he'd

done it on purpose. Things had just gotten out of hand. "I mean no."

Zane sighed. The words coming out of his mouth were not right. This apology was definitely not going according to plan. Nothing, he thought wearily, had gone according to plan since the day his stepfather had been kidnapped.

"I didn't mean to take advantage," he finally said in exasperation. "I'll see you later."

"Later," Mirabella murmured, but he had already left her bedroom.

A moment later, she heard her front door closing. The joy that had wrapped itself around her last night as she finally drifted off to sleep slipped away, leaving her feeling cold.

Zane really hadn't expected to see her at her desk today, certainly not so soon after he'd left her.

Glancing at his watch, he saw Mirabella had arrived less than an hour behind him. He thought of his sister. It took Marceline more than an hour to just shower and put on her makeup, never mind pack a few essentials and actually show up somewhere. That took his sister the better part of a morning, if not longer.

Maybe Mirabella hadn't packed, he amended. Looking around the front of her desk as he passed it, he didn't see any evidence of a suitcase.

"Where's your suitcase?" he asked her.

Maybe it was her imagination, but the very sound of his voice made her tingle.

"In my car," she answered. "I thought bringing it into the office with me would cause too much speculation."

There was only a small touch of humor in his laugh. "I think the ship has sailed on that one," he told her. "Four people have already come up and congratulated me on my 'elopement.'" He still had no idea how they knew. "Did you tell anyone?" he asked her.

Mirabella replied, "No one," with such solemnity, he saw no reason not to believe her.

"I didn't, either. Then how would anyone know?" he questioned.

Mirabella thought the answer to that was self-evident. "A corporate jet isn't exactly something you can slip into your pocket without people noticing. The pilot had to sign out the plane, register a flight plan. There're lots of ways for people to get wind of this," she pointed out as she turned on her computer, then her monitor.

How had that escaped him? "I guess you're right," he agreed. "I forgot about the jet."

With that, Zane turned away. He had some notes he wanted to pick up from his office before going to his next meeting.

"And then there's this," he heard Mirabella say as he started to walk into his office.

"Did you say something?" he asked, pausing just inside his threshold to look back in her direction.

Mirabella stared at her computer monitor. The words all but leaped out at her. Anger mingled with a feeling of hopelessness as it bathed over her.

It just didn't end, did it?

"I think I know how the rest of the staff might have found out about the wedding in Vegas," she told Zane.

Her voice sounded oddly hollow. "Something wrong?" he asked, doubling back.

Mirabella turned the monitor so he could see the screen more readily. The "Anonymous" email sender was back. Glancing at the time stamp, the email had been sent out early this morning. It was the first thing she saw when she opened her computer.

What new bridegroom is getting away with murder? the first line read. Better be careful and watch your back, Mirabella, or you might be next on his list.

Anger spiked within him. Zane bit back a number of choice words. Cursing at the sender, or at her computer, would accomplish exactly nothing. He needed to take some kind of effective action, not merely rail impotently at shadows.

Zane put his hand on her shoulder in a protective gesture.

"Don't be afraid, Belle. I'm going to track this infantile scum down. I won't let him get to you."

He meant physically, but she took it to mean mentally. "He's already gotten to me, but I'm not afraid." She fired back. "I'm angry. This jerk has no right to try to say what he's saying, to try to poison people's minds against us." Her eyes flashed as she turned them toward Zane. "What the hell is his game?"

Her normally porcelain cheeks were flushed with suppressed fury. He'd never seen her look so angry— nor so desirable. Instead of becoming incensed, which he knew was what this "Anonymous" vermin was after, Zane felt himself becoming aroused. By Mirabella.

Now wasn't the time, he upbraided himself.

It was *never* going to be the time, he reminded himself in the next moment. He'd married her to save her reputation, to squelch the hurtful, damaging rumors.

Stringing up the person saying all those caustic things about them, about *her*, did not lead to the "and they all lived happily ever after" ending he was after—even if it might prove to be immensely satisfying on a very primal level.

Nothing wrong with a little primal once in a while, Zane caught himself thinking as his thoughts returned to last night.

The next moment, because he couldn't afford to be sidetracked, he shut down both avenues of thought. The only game he needed his head in right now was the one he needed to play in order to shut this Neanderthal cretin down.

"Well, there's one way to handle this like an adult," Mirabella said to him as she poised her fingers over the keyboard, ready to delete the whole ugly mess with a couple of strokes. "And that's to not pay any attention to it."

Realizing what Mirabella was about to do, he quickly put his hand beneath hers, blocking her access to the keyboard.

"No, don't," he ordered.

Confused, Mirabella looked at him quizzically. "You want me to *save* this garbage?" Had he lost his mind—or was there something she was missing?

"Meyer's going to need the emails "Anonymous" has sent so he can trace them back to the sender. It's got to be someone within the company who's sending these emails. I think it's the same person who engineered those fake authorizations to transfer Eldridge's funds into that dummy account with your name on it. We've got a lot of sharp IT experts working for Colton Incorporated."

He paused to look at Mirabella, weighing just how to ask the next question. He'd always been a direct man. The question came out bluntly. "Do you have any enemies, Belle?"

She answered without hesitation. "I do now that I married you."

He hadn't even thought about that turn of events and didn't comment on her speculation. Besides, what she'd just said had no bearing on the timeline.

"The first email and the dummy account were set in motion before yesterday. In the case of the account, *long* before we got married," he pointed out, then tried again. "So, do you know of any enemies you might have had prior to yesterday?"

She didn't even have to think about it. Mirabella shook her head. "Nobody. I only interacted with people in the office on your behalf. In case you hadn't noticed, you've kept me very busy. Too busy to 'hang out' at the watercooler and make anyone resent me." She looked at him and asked in all innocence, "How about you? Do you have any enemies?" She saw the look that passed over his face and realized she might have accidentally stumbled onto the answer. "Who?"

Off the top of his head, he couldn't think of any one name standing out above the rest. It was more of a group deal in his case. "I'm sure I'm not on the list of favorite people when it comes to a number of former employees."

"Former employees," she repeated. It had an ominous sound to it. "As in—?"

Indulging her, Zane elaborated whom he was referring to. "People I've had to fire, either for incompetence, or for security violations. I tried to go easy on them," he admitted. "But a couple of them eventually wound up being prosecuted." Those might definitely carry a grudge, he thought. "I'd better put a list together and give it to Meyer," he said, thinking out loud.

"That would be a good start," Mirabella agreed.

Maybe once Zane got started, more names would occur to him. She just hoped they could find whoever was behind this and stop the person before they had a chance to escalate.

Mirabella stifled a shiver.

She made a good sounding board, Zane thought. But then, he already knew that. This wasn't the first time he'd bounced thoughts off her in order to decide on a course of action. He was just more aware of it because of last night, he realized.

He was just more aware of *everything* because of last night. And that was both good, and bad, at the same time.

Damn it, he had to get himself together and focus on what was important—not to mention quite possibly urgent. Matters affecting his personal life he could resolve later. But this thing in front of him could pose an immediate threat—and not just to him.

Who knew, maybe this "Anonymous" character was somehow tied up in his father's kidnapping, as well. He certainly hoped so. It would be nice to be able to wrap this up quickly.

Zane could feel his knuckles itching.

Right now, he needed to bring all this to the attention of his head IT expert. But even so, he paused for a moment longer. There were parts of his personal life he just couldn't avoid. He felt as if he needed to prepare Mirabella for what lay ahead.

"You've never met my family, have you?"

He knew it was a stilted question. There was no reason for her to have actually *met* them. She was part of another world, a world that dealt with reality and regular people whereupon his family—all of them—were a little larger than life and for the most part, definitely out of touch with the normal world.

Believing Zane was asking her a serious question, Mirabella paused to think. "Well, I've seen a number of them in passing. After all, your father and your brothers Fowler and Thomas, not to mention your sister Piper, all have offices in the penthouse," she said, referring to the top floor of the twenty-five-story glass office tower. "And I have seen your mother on occasion," she added.

That covered most of them, except for Alanna, Marceline and Reid, the former being his stepsister, just as Fowler was his stepbrother. Thomas and Reid were his half brothers. As for Piper, she was part of the family by virtue of adoption.

"*Seeing* my mother is definitely not the same thing as occupying the same space as my mother for more than a few seconds at a time." His mouth curved almost cynically. "It is an experience that leaves a deep impression on you—like being in the center of the stage during a live presentation of *You Can't Take It with You*."

She looked at him, total confusion in her eyes. The title meant nothing to her. "I'm afraid I don't get the reference. Is that a play?"

It was something he'd been forced to read in college. "A farce for the most part," he told her. "Filled with people who are a little off—but pretty much endearingly so," he recalled. "Take away the endearing part, and you've got my family."

She felt as if he was trying to warn her. "I like your stepfather," she said. He was the only one she'd had any dealings with. The others he'd mentioned she knew only by sight and only because she'd made a point of knowing them because of their connection to Zane.

"Yes, but he's not around right now."

She noted Zane said it as if Eldridge Colton was just temporarily away, like someone on a sabbatical instead of being the possible victim of a kidnapping. Or worse.

Her heart ached for Zane. He really did love his stepfather, she thought, wondering if the senior Colton was aware of that.

Without thinking, she put her hand on Zane's. When he looked at her, his eyebrows rising in silent query, she said, "He will be. You'll find him." There was no room for any dissent in her statement. She said it as if she had every confidence in the world Zane would find his stepfather.

Zane smiled at her. He knew there was no reason for her to staunchly hold to that belief, but he appreciated hearing it nonetheless.

"Thanks. Anyway, let me go talk to Meyer about this list of possible disgruntled ex-employees so he can get started checking out their whereabouts. At least it'll give us something to go on for the time being."

And after the legal means to go about an extensive search were exhausted, he was aware of the fact that the man who he regarded as his right-hand man in his security division was also acquainted with a number of so-called black hats, men and women who could—and did—hack into systems whose airtight security proved to be like the proverbial red cloak waved before a bull.

In effect, the systems presented challenges and a way to stave off boredom for them, at least for a little while.

If he had to, he would give Meyer the okay to turn to one, or more if necessary, of these men and women to track down whoever was causing him—and Mirabella—such grief and throwing their worlds into utter turmoil.

He wasn't sure just how he would decide to punish this person or persons who were creating so much damage in his life—he hadn't gotten that far. First, they had to be caught, then and only then would he allow himself to start planning a fitting punishment.

Get moving, he silently urged himself. He had to get this rolling and quickly, not just because he wanted to bring it all to an end, but because, once done, he knew he needed to get back so he could further prepare Mirabella to meet his family.

The abbreviated warning he'd given her didn't even begin to scratch the surface and he knew it. He was used to his family and their unique idiosyncrasies but for someone who had never been thrown into the deep end of the pool with these piranhas, well, it could turn out to be one hell of a shock.

And Mirabella, he had already concluded, deserved a great deal better than that.

"I'll be back as soon as I can," he told her. "Until then, don't read any more emails."

"Is that an order?" she asked, touched he was so

concerned about the effect reading these emails might have on her.

"It is a respectful request," he corrected. "And if you don't listen to that, *then* it's an order."

Chapter 17

The lighting in the IT section was deliberately dim, allowing attention to be primarily focused on whatever programming code was currently scrolling down the wide computer monitors. Carefully recruited tech experts worked like drones zeroing in on their particular targets and in this light—or lack thereof—it was difficult to distinguish one expert from another... except for Meyer Stanley.

As head of this division, not to mention the man Zane had come to rely on rather heavily as of late, Meyer's desk was set apart from the others by several feet. Not that Meyer actually took note of that fact. He was as riveted to his work, if not more so, as the others in the vast room.

The IT expert was hardly aware of Zane's presence until the latter placed a hand on his shoulder. Startled, Meyer jumped.

"Sorry," Zane apologized. "How's it coming?" he asked, nodding at the screen.

"A lot slower than either one of us would like," Meyer admitted.

The truth was something he'd never learned how to either hide or embellish on. It fell from his lips unadorned. Meyer had been far too busy learning code to take the time to learn how to lie, even for his own benefit.

"So you've got nothing new to report on the emails and the transfers?" Zane asked him, trying not to sound as disheartened as he felt.

Meyer paused to look at his boss. "Only that once we catch this guy, if you don't wind up beating him to a pulp for what he's said about you and your assistant administrator, I'd strongly suggest recruiting him for our team. Every time I think I'm closing in on this guy, the signal turns out to not be coming from where I thought it was coming. It's bafflingly encrypted, bouncing not just all over the building, but it looks like all over the immediate world. I hate to say it, but whoever this guy is, he is *damn* good."

Zane frowned, looking over Meyer's shoulder at the screen. He was into coding himself, but not to this extent. "Except for the part where he's got a completely black soul."

"Yeah, except for that," Meyer stoically agreed, remembering to put what the hacker was doing into proper perspective. "Don't worry, boss. Catching this SOB is my main priority," the man promised.

"No," Zane corrected, "right now, Meyer, catching him is your *only* priority." Zane could feel the IT expert's eyes looking at him with a hint of curiosity.

"I've got a feeling he's somehow involved in Eldridge's kidnapping."

"And the Lindbergh baby kidnapping?" Meyer quipped. It was Meyer's feeble attempt at a joke and it fell unceremoniously flat. When Zane shot him a look, Meyer could only shrug as he delivered a vague apology coupled with an explanation. "Sorry, boss, but I think that good though he is, maybe you're giving this guy *too* much credit."

If only. "And I think you're not giving him enough." Reaching into his pocket, he took out the list he'd written up, thanks to Mirabella's suggestion. "Here's a list of possible suspects to look at for this," he told Meyer, laying the list on the expert's desk.

Meyer quickly skimmed the list, and then he raised his eyes to Zane's. "These people aren't with the company anymore," he pointed out. Because he needed to monitor all employees' official communications as well as their computers, he was aware of who was currently working for Colton Incorporated, and who no longer was. "That would give whoever's doing this a working knowledge of our intranet without having to physically be somewhere in the building," he said, thinking out loud. "That adds a whole new parameter to this."

Meyer stared at his computer screen thoughtfully for a moment. "That would explain a few things," he murmured, talking to himself.

There was no point in standing around, watching Meyer type. "I'll leave you to it," Zane told him, turning away.

Engrossed, Meyer hardly heard him leave and definitely didn't hear the words.

* * *

At fifty-five, Whitney Colton was judged by many who knew her to be a handsome woman. Twenty years her husband's junior, there were others who viewed her to be nothing more than a heartless gold digger.

No one in either group, however, could deny she looked younger than her years, a fact of which Whitney was exceedingly proud, having spent a great deal of time, effort and Eldridge's money to make certain she remained that way.

Some whispered Whitney was so consumed with maintaining her youthful looks because she was having an affair with a younger man, something which, although it had been largely speculated on, had never been proved.

As for Zane, who saw his mother without the benefit of rose-colored glasses, he saw all her flaws and shortcomings clearly. He knew it was his mother's vanity, not a lover, that had her going to such long lengths and great pains not just to make the most of what she'd been given by nature, but to improve on it.

He was well aware of the fact that Whitney Colton was a rather vapid, shallow woman, but she *was* his mother and, in her own way, she had taken care of him and his sister, so he couldn't fault her completely. He even harbored, on occasion, some tender feelings toward her.

But feeling that way did not bless him with any insight into what she was thinking. For a seemingly simple woman, her thought process was rather complex in his estimation.

For one example, she was fiercely protective of the Colton name, if not so protective of any actual Colton.

Moreover, she had less than little regard for her husband's two children, Fowler and Alanna, by his first wife, Darla, and even less than that for the daughter she was forced by her husband to adopt, Piper.

Whatever actual maternal love she had to offer, Whitney divided between the four that were the actual fruit of her womb, but she did it sparingly, reigning over all of them like a queen. A queen who had clawed her way into a kingdom and meant to hang on to it no matter what it cost her—or who.

In the last six weeks, Zane had watched his mother vacillate between hysteria and over-the-top wringing of her hands as she dramatically kept vigil for the return of her Dridgey-pooh which was, in Zane's opinion, the most god-awful pet name ever conceived—and one that she had given to his stepfather.

After his less-than-satisfying visit with Meyer, Zane decided to go home to let his mother know in person what was going to take place at her dinner table that evening. This way, he hoped the histrionics he *knew* would take place could be at least diluted to some degree.

Not wanting to go into any of this, he deliberately avoided telling Mirabella about his impromptu visit home. It was bad enough to have to do it without having to *explain* he was doing it as well.

Arriving home, he cut through the ballroom-like foyer and found his mother pacing around the suite-sized living room, her designer dressing gown flowing behind her like a royal robe, marking her path. Agitation filled the very air.

When Whitney saw him enter the room, she stopped

dead in her tracks. Her expressive eyes widened with anticipation.

"What are you doing home at this time of day?" she asked, each word all but throbbing with anxiety.

"I wanted to talk to you," Zane began in a subdued voice—and got no further.

"It's him," Whitney cried, her voice quaking. She brought her fisted hand to her lips as if to absorb any cry that might escape them. "You found him. You found my Dridgey-pooh."

The second the words had left her lips, Whitney swayed, conveniently collapsing directly over one of the two sofas in the room.

Lowering her hand, she went on to dramatically clutch her chest with it as she moaned. "He's dead, isn't he? You found him and he's dead. My Dridgey-pooh is dead. Oh, why is this happening to me?" she wailed. "Why can't I just be happy?" Grabbing Zane's arm— she had a remarkably strong grip for a thin woman her age—she anchored her son to her. "Where did you find him? Will I be able to recognize him or did they do something awful to disfigure him? Why would they do—"

"We didn't find him, Mother," Zane said, raising his voice so he could cut through her keening rhetoric. He peeled his mother's fingers off his arm as gently as he could.

Whitney blinked like a person waking up from a bad dream. "You didn't?" she cried, stunned. "Then what are you doing here at this hour? Why aren't you at work?"

He would have much rather been at work, he thought. "I came to talk to you."

Suspicion immediately entered the eyes attempting to pin him down. "About?"

Why was there suspicion in her eyes? Now that she knew he had no news about his stepfather, exactly what did she think he was going to say? He really wished his mother was above suspicion—but she wasn't.

Tentatively, he began. "I want you on your best behavior at dinner tonight, Mother."

"I'm *always* on my best behavior," she informed him haughtily, insulted by his unspoken innuendo.

"*Better* best behavior, then," Zane specified, knowing what she was capable of. His mother's tongue could be sharper than a dagger, able to deliver remarks that could cut out the heart of an eagle three hundred feet away.

Whitney's eyes narrowed as she regarded her first-born. "What are you up to, Zane?"

There was no way to say it but to say it. If he waited until he brought Mirabella into the snake pit with him, her presence at the table wouldn't temper his mother's tongue. On the contrary, it just might set her off and he wanted whatever dramatics Whitney Colton intended to display to be out of her system sooner than later.

His mother at half her usual capacity was still far more than most women displayed at full capacity. He didn't want Mirabella intimidated.

In order for that *not* to happen, he knew he needed to inform his mother about Mirabella's changed marital status—as well as his own.

Taking a breath, he mentally crossed his fingers and then said, "I got married yesterday."

"You—what?" Whitney paled for a moment, and then the next moment, she waved away her son's words.

"This is not the time for you to finally develop a sense of humor, Zane. I don't appreciate the joke. Your stepfather's been kidnapped," she declared dramatically as if this was all news to him.

"This isn't a joke, Mother," Zane persisted, determined to at least get his mother to come around now that he'd gone this far. "Mirabella and I flew to Vegas—"

"Mirabella?" she echoed disdainfully as if she were repeating the name of a misnamed pet. "What sort of a name is that?"

"A beautiful one as a matter of fact," he told her with some feeling, taking offense for Mirabella. His mother had a way of tossing out insults the way a farmer tossed out feed before his nameless hens.

Anger flushed Whitney's carefully made-up cheeks. "Did she trap you? This Mirror person, did she trap you?" Whitney demanded hotly. "Is that it? Did the scheming little witch say something or do something— did she tell you that you got her pregnant?" she suddenly guessed in pronounced outrage.

"No, Mother," Zane refuted, struggling to keep his voice at an even keel. "You're projecting your own way of handling things on to her. She didn't trap me," he informed his mother. "As a matter of fact, I had to convince her to marry me."

"Convince her?" Whitney echoed in disbelief. "Why? What's wrong with her? Doesn't she have any common sense? Can't she see what a catch you are? Just what is this girl's endgame?" she wanted to know, her suspicions breeding more suspicions.

Zane glanced at his watch. He didn't have time for this. "You have about five hours to get all this negative reaction out of your system, Mother. When I bring Mirabella here tonight, I want you to welcome her, not scare her. Am I making myself clear, Mother?" he asked, his eyes pinning Whitney down.

Whitney drew herself up like a queen disrespected in her own palace. "Since when do you talk to me this way, Zane?"

He knew all her tricks. She wasn't about to get him to back down or apologize. He wasn't a boy anymore and hadn't been for some time. "Since it matters to me that you behave yourself."

Whitney sighed dramatically and rolled her eyes. "If it's that important to you, Zane, fine, bring this Mirror person on." Another worn, resigned sigh punctuated her words. "I'll make nice to the little gold digger—"

"Mother!" Zane cried sharply, letting her know he wasn't about to let her get away with this.

"Sorry, I meant the new Mrs. Zane Colton," Whitney corrected herself. She made no effort to bank down the shiver that accompanied her words, or the disdain in her voice.

"Remember," Zane warned his mother, "your *best* best behavior."

There was no humor in her smile and no affection, either. "But of course."

Biting back an annoyed sigh, Zane left the room.

Maybe he should just look into getting a house close to work, he thought, as he walked out.

He was almost out of the massive house when he decided to make a quick detour to his stepfather's bedroom—the room where the man was last seen. He knew the sheriff had been through there—as well as the grounds outside the window—not once but twice—the second time producing that cuff link. Any sort of evidence that could be found there had supposedly all been accounted for.

But given the fact that the sheriff had missed the cuff link until he'd returned to look the room and grounds over again, Zane decided it wouldn't hurt for him to do the same.

Who knew, maybe he'd get lucky.

When he came to Eldridge's bedroom, he saw his stepbrother, Fowler, was inside. And from what he could see, the president of Colton Incorporated had something in his hand. Something he was apparently trying to leave tucked behind a sofa pillow.

What the hell was going on here?

Zane said the first thing that came to his mind, though he couldn't quite believe it even as he said it. "You wouldn't be planting evidence there now, would you, Fowler?"

Startled, his stepbrother swung around to face him, accidentally dropping what he held on the floor.

Zane's eyes widened as recognition set in.

"Is that my hunting knife?" Zane demanded, stunned. It had gone missing a few weeks ago. What was it doing here, in Fowler's hands?

Moving quickly, he picked the knife up before Fowler had the chance.

Zane examined it in disbelief. "I thought I lost this. What are you doing with it?" It was more of an accusation than a question.

"I found it here," Fowler said defiantly.

Tall and imposing, with dark brown hair and intense, cold blue eyes, Eldridge Colton's thirty-five-year-old firstborn wasn't accustomed to backing down. Or to explaining himself.

Zane didn't take kindly to being lied to. "No, you're trying to *plant* it here. Why?" Then he demanded, "Why are you trying to frame me?"

Fowler shut down right before his eyes. "I don't know what you're talking about."

Fowler knew all right, Zane thought.

He knew he was going to make Fowler make a clean breast of it even if he had to beat it out of his step-brother.

"Did you kidnap him?" Zane asked angrily. "Did you kidnap Eldridge?"

"Are you out of your mind?" Fowler shot back. "Why would I harm my own father?"

Zane hadn't worked that part out yet—and to be honest, he didn't really fully believe it yet, either, but what other explanation was there for what was going on here?

"I don't know," he admitted, albeit loudly. "Why would you? You're obviously trying to throw suspicion off yourself and onto me."

"You're hallucinating," Fowler accused. "Listen, *brother*," he began, using air quotation marks around the word *brother*. "In case you've forgotten, I've got a solid alibi, remember? Breakfast table, your mother," he said mockingly, peering into Zane's face as if looking for any signs of recognition. "Any of this ringing a bell for you yet?"

Zane despised being talked down to. He'd spent half his childhood being talked down to by Fowler and he didn't intend to spend his adult years that way, or spend it idly standing by while the narcissist talked down to other members of their family.

"Watch yourself," Zane growled the warning, pushing his stepbrother back, "or I'm going to be ringing yours—and clean your clock while I'm at it."

Fowler regained his footing and adjusted his tie as if trying for an air of nonchalance.

"Careful, or I just might get it in my head to fire you."

That was an empty threat and they both knew it. "Your father won't let you," Zane countered.

Fowler's smile grew even icier. "Ah, but he's not here right now, is he? Just a word to the wise," Fowler said with an air of nonchalance.

He walked out of the room, his warning hanging in the air.

Zane ran his fingers over the hilt of the knife he'd picked up from the floor, trying to curb his anger.

In all honesty, though there was no love lost between them, Zane really couldn't picture Fowler being involved in his father's kidnapping, much less the man's possible demise. But his stepbrother was definitely trying to pin Eldridge's kidnapping on him. Why? Who was he attempting to draw attention away from?

Who was he protecting?

Fowler was a coldhearted bastard who didn't care about anyone—anyone except for Tiffany, Zane corrected himself.

Tiffany Ankler was Fowler's girlfriend and she'd been practically a fixture at the sprawling house for the past five years. It was no secret the overly endowed, statuesque blonde wanted to be upgraded to the position of fiancée. Could Fowler possibly be doing this to protect Tiffany?

Was Tiffany behind his stepfather's kidnapping for some reason?

Zane shook his head. The pool of suspects seemed to be growing instead of shrinking.

None of this made any sense, he thought, and he really needed to get back to the office. He'd already been away too long.

Maybe he should give Mirabella the option of staying at a hotel room in town instead of the house. The idea of dinner at his mother's house was becoming more and more of an ordeal in the making in his mind. But it was something that was going to have to be faced if Mirabella—as his wife—was going to be staying with him.

For better or for worse, he and all the Colton siblings called the sprawling Colton Valley Ranch mansion "home." Each of the sections they occupied were bigger in size than most people's entire houses. Eldridge's two older offspring, Fowler and Alanna, lived in the mansion's left wing while his mother and missing stepfather lived in the main house in a suite on the first floor. All the rest of them, including him, had their own suites on the second floor.

This menagerie of malcontents was what he was going to be bringing Mirabella to tonight. It occurred to him as he drove back to the office that if this hadn't been a marriage of convenience, after meeting his dysfunctional family, Mirabella might very well be tempted to file for divorce on the spot.

And he really wouldn't have been able to blame her.

His hyperdramatic mother and at least three of his siblings had that sort of effect on people.

He supposed it was lucky for him that he and Mirabella, despite the undeniable chemistry that had crackled between them last night, were married only for appearances. Otherwise, if he had actual feelings for the woman, he would seriously be worried about losing her once he brought her into the house and she saw all of them in their natural habitat.

You've got more important things to think about than Mirabella, he scolded himself.

He went on thinking about her anyway.

Chapter 18

"We are still in Texas, aren't we?" Mirabella quipped. "I mean, we haven't driven into another state or anything, right?"

They'd driven out of the city proper a while ago and had been driving for what seemed like forever. She hadn't realized the place he called home was located this far away from where he worked.

Rather than answer her question directly, Zane said, "Almost there," as he turned onto what she suddenly realized was the front drive.

The front drive appeared to be around a half mile long, if she was any judge of distance, and it led up to an ornate black iron gate. She saw Zane press something on the driver's-side armrest. Instantly, both halves of the gate swung open.

Just before it parted to admit them, Mirabella saw

the words COLTON VALLEY RANCH written across the gates in what looked like real gold letters.

A two-story sprawling mansion with an annex on either side loomed straight ahead. It looked like something straight out of a movie set during an era when every movie had been an epic.

She'd heard descriptions of the Colton family mansion, but the words used hadn't begun to do it justice. Looking at it now, it was all she could do to keep her jaw from dropping open.

"You *live* here?" Mirabella asked in wonder.

"Yup," he answered a bit stoically before sparing her a glance. "And now you do, too. As long as you're Mrs. Zane Colton," he qualified.

Pulling his vehicle over, Zane left it parked along the shoulder of the winding front drive, not too far away from the imposing double front doors. There would be someone from the household staff to take care of it soon enough.

Getting out, he came around to her side and opened the door for Mirabella.

For her part, Mirabella was still attempting to take it all in and absorb it. At first glance, the mansion looked to be bigger than the apartment complex she lived in.

"Does it come with a map?" All she could think of was how easy it had to be to get lost in a mansion of this size. Taking the hand he offered, she got out of the passenger seat, then turned toward him and put her thoughts into words. "How do you keep from getting lost?" she asked innocently.

He realized she was serious and felt his mouth curving. "You get to know your way around after a while," he assured her.

Mirabella did a quick calculation in her head. She was currently a little more than three months along in her pregnancy. That meant the baby was going to be born approximately in six months or less. How long after that before Zane would start divorce proceedings? The answer led her to an obvious conclusion.

"I doubt if I'll be around that long," she told Zane.

"We'll see" was the only answer he trusted himself to give at the moment. Taking her hand, he guided her toward the front doors. "Right now, let's just get you through dinner."

He made it sound like an ordeal. Mirabella read between the lines. "They're going to hate me, aren't they?"

Zane paused and looked at her. "I wouldn't exactly say 'hate,'" he said, feeling sorry for Mirabella. She'd already been through more than her share. Having to face his mother and some of the others seemed like adding cruel and unusual punishment to an already taxing situation.

"Let's just say some of them might not be overly thrilled at having a new face at the family table. But then," he qualified after more thought, "that bunch isn't exactly capable of initially experiencing any of the kinder emotions when it comes to interacting with someone new." He resumed walking. "Don't worry about it."

Mirabella felt queasy as she hesitated before the front doors. "Is there anything I need to know?"

"Yes," he told her honestly. "And it could fill an entire book, but it's too late to tell you any of that now."

He offered her an encouraging smile. "Just be your-self—and try not to notice when they're being them-selves," he advised.

That didn't help. "You're not going to leave me alone with them, are you?" she asked him suddenly, banking down a wave of panic.

Zane found himself laughing. "Don't worry. Even I'm not that cruel."

"I don't think you're cruel," she responded. She wasn't trying to flatter him—there was no point to that—but to just make him aware of how she felt about him as a person.

If he was going to say something to point out the error in her thinking, Zane never got the opportu-nity. At that moment, the ten-foot front door opened and a small, kind-faced woman—the family's house-keeper—welcomed them in.

"Dinner's just about on the table, Mr. Zane. You know how Miss Whitney doesn't like to be kept wait-ing." The housekeeper said his mother's name as if she'd just bitten into a piece of very sour gum and couldn't quite keep her reaction from her face. "And don't worry, there's a place set for your friend," she assured him, her eyes momentarily shifting toward Mirabella.

"Moira, this is Mirabella, my wife," he said, intro-ducing Mirabella to the housekeeper.

Moira looked dumbstruck. Recovering, she gave Mirabella a quick, warm embrace. "Good luck to you, my dear. You're going to need it." She made a show of crossing her fingers for the younger woman.

"You're the best, Moira," Zane told the housekeeper, planting a quick kiss on the woman's dry cheek.

Moira snorted. "A lot of good that does me in *this* house," the housekeeper grumbled, but it was obvious Zane's compliment had managed to hit a soft spot in the woman's heart. She eased the door shut behind them. "Go on into the dining room. The others should be there by now. Looks like you've got a full house to deal with—all except for Mr. Eldridge, of course."

Mirabella noticed the moment the housekeeper mentioned Zane's stepfather, Moira's eyes were suddenly glistening with unshed tears.

The housekeeper seemed to genuinely care about the man's well-being, she thought.

Mirabella leaned over and squeezed the older woman's hand.

"He'll turn up," she said with the same sort of conviction she tried to convey to Zane.

Moira looked a bit taken aback at the kindness she heard in the newcomer's voice. She was somewhat at a loss as to how to respond, other than to nod her head and murmur, "Of course he will," with far less certainty than Mirabella had just exhibited.

"We'd better get in there," Zane advised, hurrying his new wife along.

He didn't want to give his mother anything more to grumble about and she really did hate to be kept waiting. The fact that *she* kept people waiting had no bearing on the matter.

Last-minute concerns surfaced just before they turned the corner to walk into the dining room. Zane suddenly took her hand again, immobilizing Mirabella. Though he tried not to pay any attention to it, something oddly protective was stirring within him again.

That, along with a measure of guilt.

A sudden image flashed through his mind of feeding Daniel to the lions.

His eyes looked pointedly into Mirabella's. "Are you ready for this?"

Was she ready? No. It felt as if her nerves were having an attack of nerves. But this was something Mirabella felt she needed to get through. This was, after all, his family and she was in the eyes of the law his wife. Meeting all of them on a personal level only seemed like the logical next step in this charade she had agreed to take part in.

Besides, part of her really longed to belong to a family, even for a little while.

Even *this* family.

Right now she was the outsider and they would undoubtedly view her as such. She couldn't exactly blame them because she *was* an outsider. But that could easily change.

And the nice thing was, she thought, at least for the time being, Zane seemed to be on her side, and charade or no charade, he meant a great deal to her.

"Let's do this," she said, much the way a ship's captain might have ordered. "Full speed ahead."

Hands still joined, they walked into the dining room together.

Ten sets of eyes turned their way.

Mirabella's stomach tightened.

Curiosity could be found in five of those sets. Outright hostility, in varying degrees, could be seen in the rest.

Only the eyes belonging to the housekeeper's husband, Aaron, were entirely unreadable.

"You're late," Whitney declared, breaking the silence. She turned up a foundation-slathered cheek for Zane to kiss.

This was new, he thought, lightly brushing his lips along her cheek. His mother didn't usually wait for him to kiss her cheek before proceeding. He wondered if having Mirabella with him had anything to do with this change of behavior.

Now wasn't the time for petty bickering or confrontations.

Still, he felt bound, for Mirabella's sake, to correct his mother's admonishment because, from where he stood, he knew it was covertly aimed at the young woman beside him.

"I'm on time, Mother," Zane corrected. "You're uncustomarily early."

When his mother's sigh dismissed the challenge, he knew he was right.

Whitney was still scrutinizing Zane's companion. "Aren't you going to introduce us to your little friend, Zane?"

She was making him jump through hoops, Zane thought. His mother could have just as easily alerted the others to Mirabella's new identity.

For the sake of peace—and Mirabella—he played along. "Everyone," he said, raising his voice slightly, "this is Mirabella. My wife," he added after a short pause.

"Your what?" Marceline cried, stunned.

Her voice had risen several octaves and she looked at Zane as if she'd been betrayed. She and Zane had always been a unit within this family, they had been since the first day their mother had married Eldridge, a man Marceline still detested for her own reasons.

Alanna, Eldridge's first daughter appeared to be just as shocked. "You're kidding," she retorted.

"*He* got married?" Tiffany snapped, glaring accusingly at Fowler. She'd been doing everything possible to get Fowler to propose to her for the last five years and it was obvious she resented having another woman being the new bride at the table.

Fowler deliberately ignored her.

"Good for you," Piper declared, sounding genuinely happy for Zane.

Her congratulations were echoed by Thomas and Reid, both of whom left their chairs to shake Mirabella's hand and slap Zane on the back, offering their hearty good wishes.

Fowler grew only more sullen. "It's just an elopement, no big deal," he interjected almost defensively. His words were aimed at the woman whose eyes he was avoiding.

Whitney frowned at the duo still standing. "Sit before everything gets cold," she ordered.

She waited until both Zane and the interloper, which was the way she had labeled the woman Zane had brought to her table, were seated before speaking again.

Zane noticed his seat was arranged differently this time. His chair was on one side of his mother and Mirabella's was placed on the other. Although they were facing one another, the separation had been deliberate. His mother's unspoken message was very clear: divide and conquer.

Think again, Mother.

Once they were seated, Whitney turned to her new daughter-in-law. The smile she offered appeared forced. "Welcome to the family, dear. You're not exactly what I would have had in mind for Zane—" she began, only to have Zane cut in.

"Your *best* best behavior, remember, Mother?" Zane tersely reminded the woman who had claimed to give birth to him. He wasn't about to sit silently by and watch her reduce Mirabella to tears.

Whitney turned a deaf ear to his warning. "But as long as my son loves you, I suppose you'll do," she concluded with a smile that might have been better suited to a mother python.

"Don't you work for Zane?" Alanna asked as if she was trying to place where she had seen her stepbrother's new wife before. Her tone of voice was clearly intended to be belittling.

Mirabella raised her chin. "Yes, I do," she replied proudly, almost daring the other woman to say something else.

Alanna turned her bright green eyes toward Zane. "I guess this puts a new meaning to bringing your work home with you."

Fowler snickered at his sister's attempt at a witticism.

Zane found himself growing angry. It occurred to him the sheriff viewed all the people at the table as suspects in his stepfather's kidnapping and possible murder—and maybe the sheriff was on to something, after all. He bore no ill will toward Reid, Thomas, Piper or Marceline, but as for the others…

"I told Belle that you'd all behave yourselves, but

I guess your manners aren't up to hers," he informed the people at the table.

"Zane doesn't mean all of us," Piper said to Mirabella. "Speaking from experience, after a while, you won't even notice or pay any attention to their feeble barbs and attempts to bring you down." She looked directly at Alanna as she said, "They're threatened by anyone they see as being even remotely normal."

"That's enough. I won't tolerate any arguing at my table," Whitney announced as if she were the soul of propriety and innocence.

"Nice to know, Mother," Zane said, the look on his face daring Whitney to go back on her word.

Pressing her liberally painted Startlingly Red lips together, Whitney abruptly changed the subject and dedicated herself, for the rest of the meal, to ignoring her new daughter-in-law, an act for which Mirabella was eternally grateful.

Dinner seemed to drag on endlessly, going through a total of four courses, followed by an assortment of desserts. Mirabella was far too full to even contemplate sampling any of them, despite the fact that one of the desserts brought out was German chocolate cake, which was her special favorite.

Fowler's girlfriend had already left the table a few minutes ago, saying something about needing to walk off the calories. Mirabella suspected Tiffany was actually trying to get her anger under control. Apparently, in light of Zane's announcement, the woman had felt slighted because she hadn't gotten Fowler to the altar first.

But at least Tiffany had paved the way for her to

leave the table for a few minutes. She really needed to clear her head.

"If you'll excuse me," Mirabella said to Whitney, who was, after all, her hostess. "I think I'd like to go out to the garden to get a little air."

Forced to address her, Whitney's sharp eyes took immediate measure of her new daughter-in-law. "You look a little pale, dear," she observed coolly. "Why don't you go lie down, instead?"

"No, just a little air and I'll be fine," Mirabella assured the older woman.

She saw Zane looking her way and begin to rise in his chair, preparing to come with her. She didn't want to take him away from his family. Mirabella subtly moved her head from side to side, silently telling him to remain where he was. Right now, solitude and the night air would do her more good than anything else.

The Coltons, Mirabella realized, were best taken in small doses, at least at first. And she was close to overdosing.

As Zane began to rise anyway, Whitney clamped down her manicured hand over his, all but anchoring him at the table.

"Let the girl go, Zane. She said she'd be fine." Turning her attention back to his wife, Whitney instructed, "Go straight down that corridor all the way to the back. The terrace doors open to the patio. Take all the time you need." It sounded more like an order than an invitation.

"Thank you," Mirabella said politely.

And with that, she left the dining room.

Thomas saw the concerned look that came over Zane's face. They weren't exactly close, but he saw his older half brother as an ally in this battlefield he called a family and felt compassion for what Zane had to be going through.

Sitting next to him, Thomas leaned in and said, "Maybe she just needs to regroup." When Zane looked at him quizzically, Thomas explained. "This has got to be a little overwhelming to take in all at once."

He was indicating the area in general, but the look he gave Zane told him they were of like mind. It was the rest of the family that was overwhelming, not the house itself.

"But at least she survived the first encounter. You've got to take heart in that," Thomas pointed out.

Thomas was right, Zane thought. Mirabella had survived and survived well. It was, he told himself, a good sign.

Chapter 19

Considering the vastness of the house, Mirabella was rather surprised at how easily she found her way to the rear patio.

Like a prisoner making good her escape, she opened the French doors and stepped outside. Closing the doors behind her, she took in a deep, long breath and willed herself to just appreciate the cooler night air, making her mind a blank.

The silence compared to what she had just left behind was absolutely wonderful and for a moment, she forced herself to concentrate exclusively on that and nothing else.

Because it was evening and she only had the aid of artificial light coming from the house, Mirabella could only see so far when she looked out.

Even so, she still had the impression the Colton

property went on clear to what appeared to be infinity. Squinting, she could just barely make out the outline of several buildings which, Zane would later tell her, amounted to five barns, the stables and an old barn that had been converted into apartments—living quarters for the ranch hands.

Slowly, the sounds of the night seeped into her consciousness.

And she became aware of one other sound totally out of place from the rest.

Straining to make it out, Mirabella realized she was listening to someone talking.

Tiffany. She was listening to Fowler's girlfriend, Mirabella realized. The young woman was talking to someone. When she looked around, Mirabella couldn't see the other person. Her vision was being blocked by a hedge that towered over her by perhaps a good foot and a half.

Tiffany, Mirabella decided, had to be somewhere on the other side of the hedge.

Fowler's girlfriend was definitely talking to someone. Since Mirabella didn't hear anyone's voice answering her, she assumed Tiffany was on her cell phone.

Tiffany was obviously unaware of her—which meant she was eavesdropping.

For a second, Mirabella was undecided as to whether or not to make her presence known to the other woman. After all, Tiffany had been rather rude to her at dinner, talking down to her whenever she bothered to acknowledge her at all. Still, Mirabella had never been one to deliberately eavesdrop on anyone.

The next moment, the decision whether or not to

speak up was made for her. Tiffany, thinking she was alone, began to rant about the circumstances she felt she was forced to endure.

"I am really, really sick of all these stupid family dinners that witch keeps holding. Every time I turn around, that idiotic woman is ordering everyone to attend another one of these mindless dinners. Everyone just sits there, pretending not to hate everyone else while Whitney Colton looks down on all of us like some kind of deranged queen.

"But I've been coming to them, each and every freaking one of them, like a good little soldier, smiling at all of them as if I liked them instead of hating their guts. And where the hell has it gotten me?" she demanded heatedly.

Mirabella almost felt sorry for whoever was on the other side of this call. What could they possibly say in an attempt to calm the raving woman down?

"I'm doing everything right and I'm still not married to Fowler—I'm not even *engaged* to the guy," she wailed. "And meanwhile, his stick-up-his-butt stepbrother, Zane, brings this bimbo to dinner with him and announces to everyone that she's his wife. His freaking *wife*, can you believe it? Where's the justice in this?" Tiffany retorted angrily. "This bimbo didn't even come to *one* of these roundtable circuses and he makes her his *wife*! Somebody up there *hates* me," she all but sobbed in frustration.

Tiffany's voice was almost sad as she went on. "I was *really* sure Fowler was going to pop the question when his weirdo father disappeared—Fowler was *really* upset about it. I was there for him, all caring and everything, telling him not to worry, thinking *finally* he was going to see how much he needed me—and still *nothing!*" Tiffany spat out the word in furious disgust.

Mirabella heard her blow out a long-suffering breath. "I really love the man, but I swear he's going to make me absolutely *crazy*. Obviously, I'm going to have to do something really drastic because everything I've already tried so far hasn't gotten me anywhere."

Mirabella thought she could almost *hear* the other woman making up her mind.

"It's time to step up the ante. I am *not* going to spend one more minute than I have to waiting for that man to propose. He's going to put a rock on my hand or *else*," Tiffany threatened heatedly.

Whoever she was talking to obviously must have asked, "Or else what?" because Tiffany shouted, "I don't know *what*. But I'll think of something, I can promise you that."

Mirabella stood there, numbed by what she'd just heard.

Tiffany continued talking to whoever was on the other end of the call, but the woman had moved on in her rant and was now almost viciously criticizing what Whitney had worn to dinner. From the sound of it, Tiffany was going to go on like that for a while.

Mirabella stopped listening.

Exactly what did Tiffany mean by "everything she'd tried"? Mirabella wondered. Just what had the other woman tried? And just how was she planning on upping the ante, the way she'd just declared?

Had Fowler's girlfriend engineered Eldridge's kidnapping just to force Fowler to propose to her?

That sounded nothing short of insane, like a B movie plot that couldn't get off the drawing board, but the more Mirabella had listened to the woman's mounting rants, the more likely that possibility became.

She had to tell Zane.

Contemplating this scenario, Mirabella bit her lower lip. If she told Zane about this, she would have to own up to eavesdropping.

She was aware eavesdropping wasn't exactly a recommendable trait and was undoubtedly something a man would have viewed as a character flaw in his wife, but these were extenuating circumstances and every tiny hint of a clue she stumbled across pertaining to his father's disappearance had to be brought to light because it might just turn out to be *the* clue that led them to Eldridge's whereabouts.

Okay, she'd had more than enough "fresh air" for a while, Mirabella thought as she opened the French doors again and slowly eased herself back into the house—just in time to walk smack into Zane.

She bumped into him so hard that had he been a small-built, thin man, she would have easily knocked him backward. Instead, thrown off balance, she almost caused herself to fall.

Acting quickly, Zane caught hold of her shoulders and managed to steady her.

"Whoa there," Zane cautioned, the phrase rising to his lips automatically.

He'd been raised on the ranch. Raised on chores. None of the Coltons were spared the discipline of working with any of the animals on the ranch, especially the horses. Horse ranching was, Eldridge had maintained, in their blood as well as their birthright.

"You okay?" he asked. When she nodded her head, he dropped his hands from her shoulders. "I was just coming to look for you," Zane told her. "I thought maybe the fresh air turned out to be so enticing, it tempted you to make a break for it."

Placing an arm around her shoulders, he steered her toward the interior of the mansion.

Mirabella, thinking he was taking her back to the dining room, dug in her heels. She needed to tell him about the conversation she'd overheard and she didn't want to risk being overheard herself while she was doing it, even though, in the ultimate scheme of things, it might seem like poetic justice.

She wasn't moving. He looked at her quizzically. "There *is* something wrong," Zane concluded, noting the serious look on her face.

Instead of answering him, she asked, "Where's your room?" She was fairly certain they wouldn't be overheard there—not unless someone had actually bugged his room.

"It's more of a suite," Zane corrected. "And it's on the second floor." He searched her face, wondering what was going on. "Why?"

Still not answering, filled with the urgency of the situation, Mirabella took his hand and tugged on it despite the fact that she hadn't a clue which direction she should be going in. All she knew was she wanted to begin the process.

"Take me there," she urged.

A small, knowing laugh escaped his lips. He thought he understood what was going on. "Had enough of my family for one day, huh?"

"Yes."

The word seemed to explode from her lips of her own accord. And then she realized what it had to sound like to him. She didn't want him thinking she was attacking his family. It would make him side with them and right now, she needed to have him open-minded.

"I mean no." That wasn't right, either. She closed her eyes for a second, trying to center her thoughts. "I mean that's not it."

"Multiple choice." Zane nodded his head, as if he was making sense of her response. "Do you get to choose the right answer, or do I?"

He was aware he was teasing her and he shouldn't be, not given her expression, but right now she struck him as being adorable. He hadn't been aware of that about her before tonight.

Zane felt all sorts of emotions stirring within him, all centered on Mirabella. His thinking, he realized, was a little off. Maybe he shouldn't have had wine at dinner, he told himself.

But it took more than a glass of wine to blur his thinking. More than several glasses when he came right down to it. He had an amazing tolerance for alcohol. There was something else at play here, but for now, he avoided any in-depth self-examination. That path, he had a feeling, would only lead to trouble.

He turned his attention back to the intense-looking woman before him. "What's this all about, Belle?" He wanted to know.

"Just take me to your bedroom," she insisted.

Maybe he was overthinking this. Maybe she just wanted to be alone with him.

If so, this was decidedly a far different Mirabella than he was accustomed to.

Just what was in the meal she had consumed? he

wondered, a bit amused. He'd never seen her behave quite this way.

Without another word, he took her to his room.

"Okay," Zane said several minutes later, closing the door behind him and then turning to face her. "We're here. Now what?"

"Here" was his bedroom suite which, she thought as she looked around, in size and scope was larger than her entire apartment—with room to spare.

Taking a breath, Mirabella dove in. "When I went out to get some air, I thought I was alone, but I wasn't," she began, jumping into her narrative and hoping she made sense.

Looking at her expression, Zane suddenly leaped to what, given the breathless way she was talking, he thought was a logical conclusion. "Did one of the ranch hands bother you?" he asked sharply. Anger creased his brow. "Can you point him out?"

Fury was filling him to a level he had never experienced before when he thought of someone putting their hands on her.

Realizing he had misunderstood her, Mirabella vehemently shook her head. "No—"

He didn't let her finish. "Then he came up from behind?"

Although she wasn't accustomed to raising her voice or talking over anyone, she did both now. "No, because there was no ranch hand. I wasn't alone because I accidentally overheard Fowler's girlfriend, Tiffany, talking to someone on her cell phone."

Was that all? Relieved and at the same time annoyed at the path his thoughts had taken, he snapped,

"Fowler's birdbrain of a girlfriend is always on that cell phone of hers."

"I'm not sure she's that much of a birdbrain," Mirabella contradicted.

His eyebrows drew together in a puzzled look. Mirabella wasn't making any sense to him. "What are you talking about?"

Mirabella took another breath, trying to organize her thoughts. She felt this was serious and she didn't want to make Zane impatient with her, causing him to stop listening.

"I heard Tiffany tell whoever she was talking to that she was certain Fowler would propose to her when your stepfather was kidnapped because he was so upset about it."

Zane still didn't see where she was going with this, but he was willing to give her some latitude. "All right, so?"

Realizing this was all strictly speculation on her part, Mirabella struggled to have it come out right. "So it sounds like maybe Tiffany might have had something to do with engineering the kidnapping." She saw a look she couldn't fathom pass over Zane's face. "You know, like maybe she was trying to light a fire under your stepbrother with this crisis. Tiffany obviously knew Fowler would be extremely upset about his father being kidnapped."

"We're all upset about it," Zane reminded her.

At least, that was the impression he'd gotten from the rest of his family. Still, she might be on to something. Lord knew he'd harbored his own suspicions about the kidnapping.

"Yes, I know," Mirabella said quickly, not wanting him to think she was trying to insult his family, or cast them in a collective bad light. "Of course you are. I didn't mean to imply you weren't. It's just that I really had the impression Tiffany was so desperate to get Fowler to propose that she was willing to do anything to make it happen. And maybe, feeling that way, she might not have stopped because she had to bend or break a few rules to make it happen."

Mirabella stopped and pressed her lips together. Maybe, even though her intentions were good, she had gone too far.

"You have a funny look on your face," she observed. "I'm sorry, I didn't mean to sound like I was insulting your family—"

"Tiffany isn't part of my family," he was quick to point out. And then he stopped to think as he recalled something. "And now that you've mentioned it, your take on this could just explain some things."

"Like what?" Mirabella asked before she could stop herself.

This wasn't, after all, actually her business since she really *wasn't* part of the family—and the last thing she wanted was for Zane to think she was hunting for some sort of praise or acknowledgment. She was just trying to give him the information she had stumbled across, hoping it might lead to something.

"I caught Fowler in Eldridge's room earlier," he told her.

Mirabella's eyes widened and for a split second, his thoughts were diverted. She definitely had a way of distracting him. With effort, he forced himself to refocus.

"Fowler was trying to plant something of mine in Eldridge's room."

Because it was so foreign from her own code of behavior, Mirabella struggled to understand what he was telling her.

"You mean like with the cuff link?" Was he saying his stepbrother was trying to *frame* him? The idea seemed too odious to contemplate—and yet…

Zane nodded grimly. "Yes, except more lethal. He was planting my knife there."

"Oh." Mirabella felt as if all the air had just left her lungs.

"But now it's all beginning to make sense," he told Mirabella. "Fowler was doing it to throw suspicion away from Tiffany. He obviously thinks the way you do, that Tiffany had something to do with my father being kidnapped."

"Well, if he really does think that, maybe that's why he hasn't proposed to her. Because he's not sure what she's capable of." It didn't exactly make for a marriage made in heaven, Mirabella thought. She followed the thought further. "And if he feels that way, maybe Fowler should take his suspicions to the sheriff."

That, Zane thought, carried consequences with it. "And if he's wrong, she's never going to forgive him," Zane pointed out.

That could actually be a good thing for Fowler, Mirabella couldn't help thinking. "She didn't exactly sound like she was in all that forgiving of a mood when I heard her talking." She laughed shortly. "I don't blame him for not wanting to be on the wrong side of that woman."

Which in turn brought Zane to another thought, one

of the reasons he had gone looking for her to begin with. "Speaking of which," Zane said, "I'd like to apologize to you for my mother's behavior tonight. And, while I'm at it, for Fowler's, Marceline's and Alanna's behavior, as well."

Maybe he should have prepared her better than he had—or not brought her to dinner at all, just slipped quietly into the house after the fact. His mother would have been outraged, but her response was really not his main concern here. She could—and always would—look out for herself. Mirabella needed protecting.

"I guess it was more like a gladiator battle than a spirited family dinner," he admitted. "But, at least you've seen the worst of it." A rueful smile curved his mouth. "I'm afraid my family gives the word *dysfunctional* a bad name."

She didn't want him feeling this way. They were, after all, his family and she would make the best of it for as long as she had to put up with them. He'd married her to give her baby an established name and she owed him for that.

"They're a little rough around the edges," Mirabella charitably allowed, "but it could have been worse."

He looked at her incredulously. To his way of thinking Mother Teresa would have had difficulty finding good things to say about some of the members of his family. "How?"

"Give me a minute," Mirabella deadpanned. "I'm working on it."

Zane laughed then. Laughed and without thinking, drew her into his arms and hugged her. "You're a good sport, Belle," he said with genuine feeling.

She looked up at him, trying not to pay attention to

how his embrace seemed to unravel her. She offered him a rueful smile. "I don't exactly have much choice in the matter," she reminded him.

And neither, he realized as he slowly brought his mouth down to hers, did he.

He'd been thinking about her all day. Flashes of last night and the way it had unexpectedly unfolded insisted on replaying in his head, causing him to vividly recall every single detail of the evening he'd spent with her, acquainting himself with an entirely new and different Mirabella than the one he had become used to and thought he knew.

He'd discovered last night he'd been wrong. He *didn't* know her.

He'd been wrong, too, in thinking he knew himself inside and out, as well.

He didn't.

And it had taken one night with Mirabella to make him realize that.

Chapter 20

Nearly three weeks had gone by since he'd brought Mirabella to meet his family en masse around the dining room table and in all that time, nothing had gone according to his plans.

It still hadn't.

Despite the combined best efforts of Meyer, his IT team as well as himself, he still hadn't managed to find out the identity of the person who'd sent the vicious emails, the one who had created the dummy bank account that had been set up in Mirabella's name. However, at least there'd been some partial success. The money from Eldridge's account was no longer being siphoned off for mysterious deposits.

Also despite what seemed to be the best efforts of the sheriff's department, not to mention his own deliberate searches, Zane was no closer to discovering

242 _The Pregnant Colton Bride_

who had abducted his stepfather than he had been on that first morning when Moira's horrified scream had pierced the air and sent them all into an emotional tailspin.

Zane found himself still suspecting members of his own family, first one, then another, unable to rule anyone out from the first tier at any given time.

The only members of his family he didn't suspect were Piper, Reid and Thomas. None of them harbored a secret grudge against Eldridge, nor did any of them have anything more to gain by either their father's death _or_ his prolonged absence than any other.

As far as he could ascertain, there was no bad blood between his stepfather and any of them. Eldridge had been instrumental in arranging to adopt Piper when she was orphaned at seven, he'd made Thomas the vice president of Colton Incorporated, second only to Fowler, and he had given Reid his blessings when the latter had gone his own way to become a Dallas police detective. And although Reid was no longer on the force, the reason he wasn't had nothing to do with Eldridge.

However, Zane's suspicions about Fowler, Alanna, Marceline, Tiffany and, to some extent, his own mother, remained. He was still trying his best to separate fact from fiction and get to the unvarnished truth about each of their dealings. Zane still wasn't sure if any of them were capable of doing something as cold-hearted as kidnapping Eldridge or, worse, murdering him.

Even his resolve about his behavior toward Mirabella was not going the way he wanted it to. Each morning, as they traveled to work, he promised himself that he was going to adhere to his initial intent: this was to be a marriage of convenience existing on paper and in name only. Anything he felt for her otherwise was his problem and he was going to keep a tight rein on it.

But then evening would come and all his promises to himself from hours ago would somehow break apart like soap bubbles blown into an autumn wind. When he found himself alone with her, all the yearning, all the desire he'd been trying so hard to bury would just work its way to the surface and before he knew it, instead of keeping her at a chaste arm's length, he was promising himself "just one last time" and then, after that, he'd stick with the program.

Except he didn't.

Each "one last time" laid the groundwork for the next time, paving the way with more unspent passion and desire even stronger than it had been the night before. Consequently, despite silent promises to himself, each night found him making love with Mirabella, unable to get his fill, but still vainly hoping this time would be the charm.

It had been like that since the first night they'd spent together.

Zane woke up early and at first, instead of getting up and getting dressed the way he normally did, he propped his head up on his upturned hand and just watched Mirabella sleeping beside him.

Looking at her sleeping like that, still retaining an aura of innocence about her even after all the lovemaking from the night before, slowly began to stir him all over again.

The desire to touch Mirabella, to kiss her and hold her began to grow steadily more powerful, more demanding within him.

Zane was completely mystified. He had no idea what was happening to him. He'd never been this way before, even when he had imagined himself to be in love—

Love.

The sudden realization came out of nowhere, striking him with all the force of a head-on gale traveling ninety miles an hour.

It dawned on him why he couldn't seem to exercise proper control over himself. He was falling in love with this pretend wife of his—and that was a bad thing. Bad because this was only a temporary, practical arrangement between them, something they had both agreed upon when they'd first entered into it. He was a man of his word and that meant he would have to keep it, no matter how he felt about her.

When this was over—and by *this* he guessed that meant her pregnancy, culminating in the baby's birth—their arrangement, not to mention their cohabitation, would be over.

He needed to get some air, not to mention some distance from Mirabella as well as some desperately needed perspective, he thought.

Slipping out of bed as soundlessly as he could, Zane gathered together his clothes and carried them into the bathroom before getting dressed. He didn't want to risk making any noise and waking Mirabella up. Because if he did and she asked him where he was going, he didn't want to have to tell her "Away from you," even though it was the truth.

Zane was dressed and out of the suite in less than five minutes.

Because it was a Saturday, there was no reason for him to leave for work—which was exactly why the temptation to spend the morning in bed, with Mirabella, would have been too much for him to resist. He *needed* to resist, before staying in bed and making love with her at all different hours became too much of a habit that he both looked forward to and cherished.

Doing so would only make matters worse.

He knew what he needed to do. He needed to go cold turkey, give up all physical contact with her. This was his first step.

Not wanting to run into anyone—conversation was not high on his list—he decided to go for a ride. Before life had gotten so very complicated, he would sometimes go for a horseback ride just to clear his head.

Zane headed for the stables.

When he got there, he found the door slightly ajar. Wondering if someone else had the same idea as he did, Zane eased his way into the stables, making sure he left the door the same way he found it. Since almost everyone was still a suspect in his eyes, he wanted to see who else was in the stables before he called out to them.

Zane had the answer to his question as soon as he walked in.

Marceline was in the far end of the stable, her back to the door. His sister was facing one of the stalls and whispering, presumably to her mare, Queenie, who she doted on and rode frequently.

Memories of their childhood, when the two of them only had one another for comfort, came flooding back to him. He found himself experiencing a softening of resolve toward his sister. Maybe they could go out for a ride together, relive some of the old times, he thought, warming to the idea.

Zane was about to call out to her when he realized his sister wasn't whispering to her horse. Marceline was talking in a low voice to a man inside the stall. Zane frowned. He couldn't tell who it was or what was being said without giving himself away.

All he could actually make out was the man's dirty work boots. Marceline was talking to one of the ranch hands.

For a second, the secrecy and the covert whispers had Zane thinking perhaps Marceline, who'd told him dozens of times how much she hated Eldridge, was meeting with a fellow conspirator, plotting their next move—or maybe even discussing how they would get rid of Eldridge's body.

Hold it, get a grip. She might hate the guy, but Marceline isn't some violent, psychotic person. She certainly isn't a cold-blooded killer.

Maybe not, but then what was she doing in the stables so early, whispering with a ranch hand?

If this had been *anyone* else except for Marceline, he would have said she was in the stables for an early morning assignation with the ranch hand. At this hour, nobody would think to look for her here—and there was something exciting about making love with the threat of discovery. He knew Marceline definitely had her wilder moments.

However, the next moment, common sense prevailed, shooting down his little theory about love amid the horse stalls. Zane loved his sister, but he'd be the first to admit life as a Colton had turned her into an out-and-out snob. She would no sooner be caught in a compromising position with a ranch hand than she'd shave her head and run away to join a cult that had taken a vow of abstinence and poverty.

Most likely, Zane decided, Marceline was just asking the guy to saddle her horse—or even more likely, she was *ordering* the ranch hand to saddle her horse and also complaining about the neatness—or lack thereof—of the stable. Knowing Marceline, she was making the poor guy's life miserable.

Zane stepped back into the shadows before she could look his way and discover his presence.

Now that he thought about it, he recalled recently seeing Marceline coming out to the stables a couple of times before, always at an early hour, always smiling a little self-satisfied smile. Was it that she enjoyed making this particular ranch hand's life miserable, or didn't it matter to her who was on the receiving end of her sharp tongue?

Unless there was another reason for her being out here…

If he came right out and asked her, Zane knew how his sister would react. Marceline would accuse him of stalking her and that wouldn't get him anywhere. It definitely wouldn't answer his question or alleviate any of his suspicions.

But Zane promised himself that he'd keep an eye

on Marceline, just in case there was more going on here than it appeared.

It was the same promise he'd made himself when it came to the others on his active suspects list.

This was, he decided, going to get tricky.

He regretted not having more people he could trust.

Stymied in both fields he was looking into and pursuing, and making far more headway in the one area where he had promised to hold himself in check, Zane was not in the best of moods when it came to dealing with some of the less likable members of his family. His temper, he found, had become almost alarmingly short.

The next evening, long after dinner was over, his path unexpectedly crossed Fowler's when he was looking for a book in Eldridge's library.

Fowler looked at him with a condescending smirk and asked, "So, how's that little number you hooked up with performing in bed? Did she turn out to be a huge disappointment, or is she a case of still waters running deeper than a mud puddle?"

Walking past him, Zane chose to simply ignore his stepbrother—or at least he tried to. But Fowler was not above regressing to behavior he'd displayed while they'd grown up: bullying his younger stepbrother for his own perverse satisfaction.

Hitting Zane's shoulder with the flat of his hand, Fowler's tone was nothing short of belligerent as he angrily said, "Hey, I'm talking to you! Don't pretend you didn't hear me."

Fowler went to hit his shoulder harder, only to have Zane block the blow and deliver one of his own. Startled and unprepared for the counterassault, Fowler stumbled backward.

"I was trying to ignore you because if I didn't, I was going to wind up doing this."

Before Fowler could respond, Zane swung his fist back and then made contact with his stepbrother again, this time hitting Fowler square on the jaw. Fowler grabbed hold of the shelves behind him to steady himself.

"Now back off," Zane warned ominously, "or I'm going to sic the sheriff on your girlfriend."

Fowler's head snapped up, his eyes instantly alert as they searched his stepbrother's face. He took care to keep his distance, staying out of the range of Zane's arms as he glared at him.

"What the hell are you talking about, Zane?" he demanded.

Was Fowler serious? "You didn't think I'd figure out why you planted that cuff link outside your father's bedroom window? Or why you were trying to plant my knife in his room when I walked in on you? You were trying to make the sheriff think I had something to do with your father's kidnapping so he wouldn't look too closely at your little gold-digging, vapid girlfriend for the crime."

If it hadn't been a physical impossibility, Zane would have said there was steam coming out of Fowler's ears.

"You're crazy!" Fowler cried.

"Am I?" Zane asked calmly. It did his heart good to see Fowler's agitation growing the quieter his tone became. "Tell me you haven't thought about it yourself," he accused. "Tell me you don't think Tiffany's capable of kidnapping your father, maybe even killing him, just to get you to do what she wants you to do."

Fury colored Fowler's complexion, making it a bright red. "You don't know what you're talking about," Fowler protested heatedly. "Tiffany wouldn't do anything like that."

"If you really believe that—and you didn't do anything to Eldridge yourself—" Zane qualified as he began to lay out his theory.

"You're a lunatic!" Fowler yelled, cutting in. He turned the argument around, pointing a finger at Zane. "Maybe *you're* the one trying to frame other people. Maybe *you're* the one who kidnapped Dad, maybe even killed him, and now you're trying to blame someone else."

The only thing Zane was sure of at this point was he *hadn't* kidnapped or harmed his stepfather, but given the pronounced agitation on Fowler's face, maybe accusing him and that annoying girlfriend of his was going a bit too far. Fowler really looked as if he was becoming unhinged. To be completely honest, he had no idea what Fowler was ultimately capable of in a distressed, devolved state.

So Zane decided, at least for the time being, he'd let the matter drop. Getting into a shouting match with Fowler wasn't going to solve anything, nor was it going to lead to any productive conclusions. It might even wind up being harmful.

Not for the first time, Zane thoroughly regretted his mother had ever gotten involved with Eldridge Colton and married the man. That one act wound up effectively joining him as well as Marceline with these unbalanced, insane people, namely his stepbrother and stepsister.

Forgetting about the book he had set out to find, he felt he had no choice but to go up to his suite…and Mirabella. He'd been stalling, hoping she would be asleep by the time he got up there, but at this point, he didn't want to wind up running into anyone else. He just wanted to get some sleep and forget his last name was legally Colton, thanks to Eldridge having adopted him—and Marceline—when the man married his mother.

Reaching his suite, he glanced at his watch. It was almost midnight. Mirabella would be asleep by now— wouldn't she?

When he walked in, he found Mirabella was indeed in bed and at first glance, he thought he'd lucked out. She appeared to be asleep.

But appearances could be deceiving.

"Hi," she murmured as he began stripping off his clothes. "I thought maybe you'd decided to go back to the office instead of coming to bed."

He had entertained that idea, but there was no point in saying so. She'd only put the wrong meaning to his words. He wasn't avoiding her so much as he was avoiding himself—or at least his reaction to her.

Suppressing a sigh, Zane shrugged out of his shirt and sat down on the edge of their king-size bed. "No, I tried to find a book in Eldridge's library."

She'd noted he had come into the bedroom empty-handed. Being careful never to assume too much when it came to Zane, she asked, "You didn't find it?"

Zane dragged his hand impatiently through his hair. "I found Fowler instead," he told her.

That didn't sound good, she thought. "And?" she asked, urging him on.

"And I should have come up to my bedroom instead of looking for the book. *Our* bedroom," he corrected, realizing his error. He looked at her, wondering if he'd hurt her feelings.

Mirabella didn't want him feeling guilty about such insignificant oversights. In the three weeks she'd lived in the mansion, she had come to have somewhat of a tougher skin. She no longer saw a slight hiding behind every sentence, every look.

She knew this was all only an interlude in her life, but while it continued, she was going to make the most of it and enjoy the shreds of happiness she came across. And she was going to enjoy being with Zane for however long that lasted.

"At any rate, you're here, now," she said, pointing out the bright side of the situation.

It was, Zane thought, typical of Mirabella. She had a tendency to gravitate to the upside of things. It was something he had come to really like about her.

"Why don't you come to bed and get some rest?" she suggested. "It's almost tomorrow and you've got a full day scheduled."

Zane looked at her. He knew if he got into bed, it wouldn't be rest he'd wind up seeking. It would be, he realized, solace.

She was his solace.

He began to wonder why he was fighting it—and himself—so hard. If he felt he didn't deserve happiness, well, that was an argument for another time. Right now, he was tired of resisting.

He wanted her.

"You know," he told her, "that sounds like a very good idea."

Stripping off the remainder of his clothes, Zane got into bed.

And found the peace that had been eluding him all day.

Chapter 21

"Why haven't they *found* him yet?" Whitney demanded, looking from Zane to the young woman she was just barely beginning to tolerate. "Where *is* my Dridgey-pooh?" she cried, her voice quavering in dramatic frustration.

Because a part of him felt sorry for his mother, spurred on by a latent sense of filial obligation, Zane had opted to have dinner at home tonight rather than a restaurant in Dallas.

They were alone at the table tonight, he and Mirabella, along with his mother. The others were all absent for one reason or another, having made their excuses via phone calls.

His mother, Zane observed, scarcely seemed to notice the others were missing from the table. She was completely beside herself as yet another one of the private detectives she'd hired had returned to her with nothing to show for his efforts but empty verbiage and unsubstantiated promises that he'd locate her missing husband "very soon."

Exasperated, Whitney had fired the man on the spot. That made three private detectives since her husband had disappeared. Three detectives hired and fired with nothing to show for it.

Morose, Whitney had barely touched her dinner, moving the slices of prime rib around on her plate as if they were engaged in some sort of endless race they were destined not to win.

Her eyes growing watery, Whitney turned them toward her son. "I don't understand. How does a man just disappear like that?" she cried.

Zane knew better than to attempt a serious answer to her question. No logical or practical explanations would even *begin* to satisfy his mother.

There was only one thing she wanted to hear, so that was what he offered her. "You'll find him, Mother. It's just a matter of time."

Grateful for the slender lifeline he had thrown her—never mind that it was unsubstantiated—Whitney covered his hand with her own, her perfectly lacquered scarlet nails clicking against the tabletop.

"You think so?" she sobbed. Pausing to dab at the corners of her eyes, she looked every inch the concerned, grieving wife.

Almost too much so, Zane thought. But then, the word *easygoing* had never been included in the same sentence as his mother's name.

"You *really* think so?" she pressed, her voice spiking

up to the level of a squeak as she apparently clutched at the flash of hope Zane's words created for her.

"Yes, I do," Zane assured his mother with practiced patience.

"You really think your stepfather will just turn up?" Mirabella asked him some thirty minutes later as they left Whitney sipping brandy in the living room.

"Honestly?" He paused on the way up to their suite. "I don't know," he told her. "I was just telling her what my mother needed to hear."

To the outside world, Zane had presented a reserved, distant front, but in her heart, she had always known there was a softer side to him that he held in check.

"That's very sweet of you," Mirabella said. "You were trying to comfort her."

He wasn't about to take credit when he didn't deserve it—at least, not all of it. "Yes and no," he corrected. "Mainly, I was trying to give her enough rope to hang herself."

Reaching the landing, Mirabella stared at him. She was officially lost and confused. "Then you *don't* believe your mother's innocent," Mirabella guessed, trying to get a handle on his thinking.

Was he supportive of his mother, or did he suspect her? She couldn't tell from his tone.

He paused by their suite's door. Ordinarily, he didn't talk about what went on in his family, not out of any sense of misplaced loyalty, but because it wasn't anyone else's business. He didn't look at Mirabella in the same way he looked at everyone else. In the last three weeks, almost without his knowledge, she had come to mean a great deal to him. He'd gotten close to her without meaning to.

"She's my mother but that doesn't mean I think that makes her above suspicion. The way she's carrying on, it's like watching a performance of the poor man's *Macbeth*." He smiled and quoted one of the play's key lines. "The lady doth protest too much."

"Then you do think she's guilty," Mirabella concluded as she walked into what she regarded as their sanctuary.

"I think she's playing the wounded queen and, being my mother, she's playing it up to the hilt." When Mirabella looked at him quizzically, he elaborated. "My mother has always loved being the center of everything and she's always loved drama. Very honestly," he confessed, "I don't know what to believe. Is she doing this for show, because she's really concerned about my stepfather, *or* is she doing it to throw suspicion off herself? With my mother, you just never know."

"She could just be a very good actress," Mirabella pointed out.

There was always that, Zane thought. "Quite possibly," he agreed out loud.

"Or," Mirabella continued to theorize, "she could actually love your stepfather and be sincerely worried about him. These dramatic displays might just be the only way she has of coping with things."

Zane suppressed an amused laugh. He looked at Mirabella, shaking his head. "You always see the good in everyone, don't you?" he marveled.

She shrugged and an almost shy smile slipped over her lips. "It's too depressing any other way."

Mirabella was, he thought, too good to be true. And

while there was a part of him that had always viewed such occasions—and such people—with a very jaundice eye, Zane found himself believing in this woman who always found something positive to say about everyone.

For just a split second, he really wished he could be like her. But that wasn't possible in the world he lived in where being suspicious was the only way to survive.

"How about your baby's father?" he asked suddenly, thinking of how they had wound up together. Mirabella had stirred his curiosity. "What's his upside?"

She only hesitated for a moment before answering. "If it wasn't for him, I wouldn't be waiting to give birth and all births are minor miracles."

He laughed drily. "I know some people who would disagree with that."

He was right, of course, but that wasn't her way. "Then those people are destined to be very sad people," she told him.

"What if he comes back?" Zane asked as the thought occurred to him.

He was aware he should be leaving this alone, that it was her business and he had no right to pry. If the tables were turned, he wouldn't have appreciated her asking him questions. But there was something within him that just wouldn't let this go.

"After you have the baby," Zane pressed, "what if he turns up again and says he wants to be part of the baby's life?"

Mirabella avoided making any eye contact. "That's not going to happen."

She seemed fairly sure of that, Zane thought. But he wasn't.

"But what if it *does*?" he insisted. "What then?" She had to consider the possibility. Consider it and have a plan.

Mirabella sighed. She hadn't wanted to talk about this, but she sensed Zane wasn't about to drop the subject.

He was leaving her no choice.

"It's not going to happen," she repeated in a tight, stoic vice, "because he's dead."

It wasn't an answer Zane had expected. For a second, he thought he'd misheard her. "What?"

Mirabella braced herself inwardly before beginning. Her voice was very still and devoid of all emotion.

"After I told him that I was pregnant, he told me if I thought he was going to, as he put it, 'ante up' with money to raise the baby, then I was even dumber than he thought I was."

Fury spiked suddenly within Zane. "Are you sure he's dead, because if he isn't—"

"Three weeks later, he died in a car accident," she said, completing her narrative. And then she looked up at him and asked quietly, "Does that answer all of your questions?"

Rather than say yes or no, Zane took her into his arms and just held her.

"I'm sorry you had to go through that," he whispered against her hair.

I'm not, because for however long it lasts, it brought you into my life, she thought.

But she knew if she alluded to anything of the kind, she would cause Zane to back away immediately, so instead, she merely shrugged in response.

"People go through worse things," she told him.

"Still doesn't make it right," he insisted, holding her.

And he found himself really wanting to make it right for her. Against all common sense, he went with his gut instincts and lowered his mouth to hers.

The rest evolved naturally.

"I think this might be your man, boss," Meyer announced several days later as the IT expert walked into his office to give him an update.

Ordinarily, if he had nothing or had merely eliminated another name on Zane's list, Meyer would send him an email or make a phone call. But this time, he wanted to give Zane the news in person.

Zane looked up sharply, instantly alert. "You mean the one who's been sending out those degrading emails?"

Meyer didn't smile very often. But now he was grinning ear to ear. The name on the piece of paper he was holding represented the culmination of a great deal of work.

"One and the same," Meyer replied proudly. There was grudging admiration in his voice as he said, "And he really is damn good."

"How did you find him?" Zane asked. He knew he had given Meyer a list of possible culprits, but the distance between being a name on a list and zeroing in on the one person who was responsible was huge.

Meyer was only too happy to explain. "The thing about computer experts who are damn good, they get too cocky, think no one's as smart as they are and they eventually make a mistake. This guy was no different."

Because he knew Zane didn't appreciate dramatics, he filled in the rest of it quickly. "I cracked his code and hacked into *his* computer. You were right to think it was a former employee," Meyer told him. "'Anonymous' was an IT expert VP you had to fire last year for multiple breeches of ethics.

"From what I hear, the sheriff was supposed to bring him up on charges, but the guy conveniently gave him the slip. The good sheriff is more of a meat and potatoes kind of guy," Meyer continued. "To him real crimes punishable by the law fall under the categories of homicides and stealing property. The sheriff defines property as something you can hold in your hand. Bottom line, this guy you fired got off scot-free. And he obviously held a grudge."

"Who is this supreme pain in my butt?" Zane wanted to know.

"Howard Kurtz," Meyer said, proudly placing the report he'd written up in front of Zane. "Name ring a bell?"

"Not offhand." Zane was trying to picture the man when he heard a sharp intake of breath coming from his doorway.

Turning, he saw Mirabella standing there. She'd just walked in to drop off several pages for him to sign and stood frozen in the doorway.

She looked white as a sheet.

Zane was on his feet instantly. "Belle, what's wrong? Is it the baby?"

But she shook her head from side to side, unable to speak for a minute. And then she found her voice just as Zane reached her.

"I *know* him," she said, looking from Zane to the IT expert who had brought Zane the news.

"You *know* Howard Kurtz?" Zane asked, still trying to summon a picture of the man in his mind. "How do you know him?"

It was hard for her to believe the rather unremarkable man was capable of something so hateful. "He asked me out on a date a few times and became very indignant when I turned him down. He called me a few choice names—and then he asked me out again. He wouldn't let up no matter how many times I said no—and then he just disappeared. I was so relieved, I never asked anyone what happened to him. I just assumed he was promoted to another department—and found someone who agreed to go out with him," she added. She'd been in time to overhear what Meyer had said just before he revealed Kurtz's name. "You fired him?"

Zane finally remembered what the man looked like—as well as the circumstances behind Kurtz's dismissal. "Had to. He didn't steal from the company—although I had a feeling it would only be a matter of time until he did—but he had bent more than his share of rules and committed several breeches of ethics.

"When I confronted him with what I'd found, he apologized, swore he'd never do it again. I'm willing to give someone a second chance, but I just didn't trust him. There was something about—"

"His eyes," Mirabella said, vigorously nodding her head as she guessed what Zane was going to say. "They were flat when they looked at you, like he didn't have a soul."

Zane laughed drily. "Well, that's one way to put it." He was going to say the man appeared to be shifty.

Turning his attention to Meyer, he asked the IT expert, "You're sure about this?"

Meyer nodded. "Initially, it was a process of elimination. When I finally zeroed in on his name, I made it my business to hack into his computer. For a clever guy, he was really sloppy. I found copies of the emails that went out about you and Mrs. Colton—except she wasn't Mrs. Colton then," Meyer amended, sparing an apologetic glance in Mirabella's direction.

"You don't have to be that exact," Zane told him, waving away Meyer's correction. "As long as you're on target with this Kurtz character—"

"I am," Meyer assured him with the enthusiasm of a man who was confident he had achieved his goal.

That was all Zane needed to hear. "Then we're good. Get me a current address on this guy, Meyer. Apparently I was too easy on him last time. I should have followed up, made sure the sheriff went after him when he slipped away. It's time Kurtz found out there are definite consequences for his actions." He glanced toward Mirabella, his expression hardening. "He needs to know he can't just try to ruin people's lives and get away with it."

Meyer's grin became wider as he took out a second sheet from his pocket and placed Kurtz's address in front of Zane. "That's his current address. He's been playing musical motels, but that's the one he's staying in right now."

"Knew I could count on you," Zane said, picking up the paper and rising to his feet.

"What are you planning to do?" Mirabella asked.

What he wanted to do was draw and quarter the

man. "I'm not sure, yet. I'll know when I get there," he told her.

What Kurtz had done was despicable, but she didn't want Zane retaliating by doing something he'd regret later. "Shouldn't you go to the sheriff with this?" It was more of a veiled suggestion than a question.

"And say what? That Kurtz sent some damaging emails? I doubt the sheriff will do anything about that—even after he stops laughing. No, I think my best option is to go confront 'Anonymous' in person—and make it very clear to Mr. Kurtz that if he ever even *thinks* about doing something like it again, he's going to have to figure out how to type emails without any fingers."

She looked at Zane uncertainly. "You're not planning on breaking all his fingers, are you?"

In his present frame of mind, he would have loved to vent his anger actionably, but he knew he couldn't. "No, but for men like Kurtz, just the threat of being subjected to some sort of bodily harm is enough to get them to back off."

Mirabella wanted to believe Zane when he said all he wanted to do was threaten the man, but she wasn't a hundred percent certain he could control his temper once he confronted the former IT expert.

It wasn't that she cared about Kurtz's welfare, but she did care about Zane and she didn't want him doing anything that could have him running afoul of the law. From what she'd gleaned, the sheriff already wasn't too keen on him.

"I'd like to go with you," she said just as he was about to leave.

"What for?" he asked, surprised.

She thought fast. Zane wouldn't react well to hearing her say she thought having her there would keep him in line. "Well, those emails were aimed at me just as much as they were aimed at you. I just want to be there to hear him apologize for what he's done."

He wanted to tell her to stay out of it, that he didn't want her being around that kind of vermin, but he knew he didn't have the right to impose his wishes on her. Charade marriage or not, Mirabella was her own person and had as much right as he did to be there when he made Kurtz accountable for what he'd done.

"Okay," he reluctantly agreed. "But you're not to do anything without my say-so. Agreed?"

"Agreed," she responded quickly.

He had his doubts, but he had no choice. He took her along.

Chapter 22

Howard Kurtz had a gambling addiction that had
gone from being a minor nuisance to a major problem
in the last eighteen months. A major problem aggravated by the fact that, because of certain underhanded
dealings he had engaged in, he had lost his job with
Colton Incorporated. Although he had managed to escape doing any prison time for his offenses, his trans-
gressions were a matter of record within the legitimate
technical world. It thereby prevented him from getting any sort of gainful IT employment with any other
major corporation.

To support his growing habit—and remain alive—
Kurtz was forced to hack into various computer systems, funneling funds into dummy accounts he'd set
up for himself under an assortment of stolen identities.

All the while, Kurtz had been harboring a major

grudge against Zane Colton for firing him from a position that had assured him a fast rise up the internal security ladder with the promise of a sizable financial reward waiting for him when he reached that goal.

As an added insurance policy, Kurtz had thought to get an in with Zane's office by getting close to his administrative assistant. The little uptight witch had thrown him a curve by turning him down when he asked her out. Frustrated, he doggedly kept after her, thinking to wear her down—only to have everything blow up in his face when Zane fired him.

Forced to go into hiding to avoid all the people he owed money to, for the last year he'd been living in one motel room after another. And all the while, Kurtz had sworn to get his revenge against the two people who had forced him into this fugitive low-level lifestyle.

But he was getting frustrated and bored with what he was doing. It all seemed too mundane and pedantic for a man of his intellect and skills. There had to be something bigger, something more *damning* he could instigate. Slowly, he began to devise a plan.

Everyone knew the old man had gone missing, which meant Eldridge had either been kidnapped—or maybe someone had killed him.

Kurtz rather relished the idea. The world would be far better off with one less Colton in it, the former IT expert thought. It would also be better off if another Colton was found guilty of that crime.

A crafty, oily smile slid over Kurtz's lips as he began to relish the idea that had started forming in his head.

Suspicion regarding the old man's fate, he'd heard, was ricocheting back and forth amid the Coltons, along with several other suspects. Given that scenario, how difficult would it be to frame Zane? He knew Zane had already been brought in for questioning once by the sheriff.

Orchestrating a second round of questioning wouldn't take much.

Staring at his laptop screen, Kurtz had begun to formulate a plan that would get rid of Zane once and for all, when he thought he heard someone knocking on his door. Instantly alert—no one was supposed to know where he was currently holed up—Kurtz felt his adrenaline racing through his veins.

He'd hidden his tracks so well, the people who were after him couldn't have found him, not this quickly, he reasoned, doing his best not to allow his panic to take control.

He heard the knock again. It was more urgent this time.

"This is the motel manager," a gruff voice outside his door announced. "Lady downstairs called to say there's water leaking from the ceiling in her bathroom. I gotta come in and check out the source. If you don't open the door, I'm gonna have to use my passkey."

Grumbling under his breath, Kurtz got up from his desk. He checked his pocket before he shuffled to the door. It was still there, he thought, absently patting the item he always kept close to him.

"Make this quick," he ordered, flipping the lock and opening the door.

"I'll make this so quick, your head'll spin," Zane promised, pushing the door back hard with the flat of his hand.

Startled, Kurtz's eyes widened as he stumbled back-

Kurtz's eyes darkened. That wasn't what he wanted to hear.

"From where I'm standing, I'm holding all the cards, jackass. You don't want to get me angry, now, do you?" he taunted malevolently.

Mirabella whimpered, momentarily diverting both men's attention to her. "I think I'm feeling sick," she mumbled, swaying.

"If you're going to throw up, make sure you aim that pretty little mouth of yours in his direction, honey," Kurtz ordered.

Anticipating the man he held responsible for the state of his plight being on the receiving end of Mirabella's vomit, Kurtz momentarily lowered his blade from her throat in order to turn her head toward Zane.

Just then, Mirabella sank down, pretending to faint.

With the knife no longer pressed dangerously against her throat, Zane lunged at the other man, grabbing hold of the assailant's wrist as he tried to get the weapon away from him.

The only "muscle" Kurtz possessed which saw regular exercise was his brain. Otherwise, despite his rage, he was impotently weak. He proved to be no match for Zane, who easily overpowered and subdued him.

Considering his condition, Kurtz did manage to put up some sort of a fight, but it was so short-lived, it was practically nonexistent. Zane was the easy victor, twisting Kurtz's arms behind his back as he got the man down on the floor.

"Let me go!" Kurtz demanded, vainly trying to pull his arms away from Zane's grip.

"Not a chance," Zane answered. Out of the corner

of his eye, he saw Mirabella scrambling to her feet to stand out of the way.

"Let me go!" Kurtz demanded again. "The sheriff's not going to arrest me for sending out a bunch of emails," he spat out.

"No, but he will arrest you for hacking into one of my stepfather's bank accounts, threatening Mirabella with bodily harm and transferring funds out of it into an account *you set up*."

"An account with your *bride's* name on it," Kurtz countered. "If they arrest anybody, it'll be her!" he almost shrieked.

"Your forensics fingerprints are all over it," Zane calmly informed him. It wasn't easy controlling his tone when he wanted to shout into Kurtz's face, but he'd noticed the calmer he spoke, the more agitated it seemed to make the other man.

There was barely suppressed fury in Kurtz's brown eyes. "Good luck in proving that," he taunted, confident in his ability to have hidden his trail.

Zane merely smiled, like a man harboring a secret. "Meyer said you'd be full of yourself."

Kurtz looked at him, confused. "Meyer? Who the hell is Meyer?"

"Meyer Stanley," he told the disgraced employee. He'd brought Meyer in from another department when he discovered how good the man was at tracking down hackers trying to get into their system. "That's the name of the man who can hack rings around you, Kurtz. The man who ultimately took you down."

Zane looked over toward Mirabella. He had to admit she seemed none the worse for this ordeal. He realized she hadn't felt faint, she'd only pretended to be to get Kurtz off his guard. He had to admit, she'd surprised him. Again.

"You all right?" he asked Mirabella, just to be sure.

"Never better," she answered as she took out her cell phone.

"Get the sheriff on the phone," he told her. He looked at Kurtz, relieved at least this part of the chaos that had become his life was over. "Tell him Christmas came early this year and we've got a package for him."

"Well, looks like that finally answers the question of who was taking all that money out of your stepfather's bank account," Mirabella said with a relieved sigh as she leaned back in the passenger seat of Zane's sedan.

It was more than an hour after the sheriff had arrived and arrested Kurtz. They had both given their statements to Watkins and once the sheriff was satisfied he had the story, he had waved them on their way.

Reviewing the circumstances, Zane laughed drily. "For a hard-nosed guy, Watkins didn't turn out to be half-bad," Zane commented. "Some men don't take kindly to being proven wrong in public."

Why was he looking at her as he said that? Mirabella wondered. Was there some sort of a hidden message in that? If there was, it was eluding her.

What wasn't eluding her was that with the author of those awful emails uncovered and on his way to jail, the need to continue their charade of a marriage was no longer really necessary.

It was over.

The thought filled her with sadness. Telling herself

not to cry, she turned her face away and looked out the side window, watching the scenery pass by.

"You're awfully quiet," Zane observed after a few minutes.

Mirabella had never been a chatterbox, but she did do her share of talking. He would have thought discovering who was behind the emails *and* the phony bank transfers would have had her voicing her elation and being more talkative, not less.

When she made no response to his observation, he asked, "What are you thinking?"

She took a deep breath, then answered, "I'm thinking you're free."

"Free?" he questioned, confused. "What do you mean 'free'?"

"Free," she repeated with emphasis. "Free from having to continue with this charade that we're married. Now that Howard won't be sending out any more of those vicious emails pointing a finger at you, you're free to tell people you're not the father of my baby— which means you don't have to stay married to me any longer. You can get on with your life."

He slanted a glance at her, trying to read her tone. "Is that what you want?"

She wanted to shout no, of course not, she wanted to stay married to him. Not just until the baby was born, but forever. But that wasn't fair and she didn't want to make him feel guilty enough not to take his freedom. So instead, Mirabella told him, "I want whatever you want."

Part of him felt he should just let it go at that. He was a Colton and he didn't strip his soul bare for anyone. But he also knew this was the best thing that had every happened to him and he risked losing it all because of pride. Pride was poor comfort in the dead of night when he was alone.

Deciding to take a risk, Zane pulled over to the side of the road, turned off his engine and said, "You want to know what I'm thinking?"

"What?" she asked hesitantly, afraid of what she might hear.

"I'm thinking, as strange as it might sound, I'm actually kind of glad I fired Howard Kurtz to begin with."

"Because he was unethical," she said, nodding her head.

"No, because if I hadn't fired him, he wouldn't have been angry enough to try to get revenge by sending out those emails." He saw her looking at him quizzically, but he pressed on. "And, if he hadn't done that, then I wouldn't have volunteered to marry you and give the baby my name. Because," he continued, taking a breath, "if I hadn't done that, then I never would have discovered I was only living half a life. More than that, I would have never discovered I was actually capable of feeling happy." He ran the back of his hand along her cheek, thinking how fortunate he was that she was in his life. "Not just feeling happy," he finally said, his voice dropping down to almost a whisper, "but feeling love, as well."

Mirabella stared at him, certain she was either hallucinating, or had somehow fallen asleep and was dreaming. "What?"

"You really want me to go through the steps again?" he questioned, amused. "Because I will if you want me to, or I could just go with the shorter version."

"The shorter version?" she repeated, confused.

"Yes," Zane said. "It goes like this."

Taking her into his arms, he brought his mouth down to hers and kissed her. Kissed her as if he had just discovered she was his salvation and he'd realized there was a real threat of losing her.

Drawing back just a little, but still holding her, he told Mirabella, "I don't want to end the marriage, Belle. I want to start it. I want to do it right and in earnest. It's the best thing that's come out of the whole crazy, miserable business that's been going on since Eldridge disappeared. I've never felt like this before and I never will again if I lose you. Don't make me lose you." It wasn't a request, it was a plea. "I mean, if you don't care about me, I won't make you stay—"

"Not care about you?" Mirabella echoed incredulously. How could he even *think* that? "And here I thought you were supposed to be so perceptive."

"Then you do care?" he asked, almost afraid to believe he could be so lucky.

Instead of answering his question, she smiled as she asked, "Could you run that short version by me again?"

A smile came into his eyes. "With pleasure," he told her.

And as he had always maintained, Zane was a man of his word. He went over the short version for her again—with pleasure.

Epilogue

Things were getting back to normal. As normal as they could be, Mirabella thought, with the founder of the company, Zane's stepfather, still missing, presumed kidnapped and just possibly, worse than that.

But missing or not, work went on, people still had to earn and draw their paychecks and she still had a job to do as Zane's administrative assistant. Wife or no wife—and she now felt like one in every sense of the word—she was still his multitasking right hand, which meant each day was filled from end to end with things she needed to get done.

Mirabella couldn't have been happier.

Even her body had stopped rebelling against her. She was no longer horribly nauseous, fighting the overwhelming desire to throw up 24/7. Quite the contrary, she had even begun to look forward to eating again, the way she used to.

And, not to be underestimated when accounting for her peace of mind, it was a relief to be able to open her computer and know there weren't going to be any venomous emails waiting for her. There was still a preponderance of emails to wade through during the course of each day, but she no longer had to worry whatever she opened was going to be painfully humiliating, or at the very least, hurtful.

Skimming through the list of that day's new emails, Mirabella came to one that gave her pause. She didn't recognize the sender, at least, she didn't recognize the user name, but it was the subject line that had her suddenly wondering if someone else had taken up Kurtz's dropped baton.

The line read: For Your Eyes Only.

Maybe it was just a sales pitch that had somehow managed to get through safeguards and firewalls, although she would have found it rather surprising. Meyer had been put in charge of the company's internal communications system and she was fairly confident nothing got by the man.

Maybe this was a legitimate email dealing with a subject that needed to be kept confidential.

"Stop speculating and open the email. You know you're never going to find out what it is until you open it, Belle," she lectured herself.

Taking a breath, she tapped on the email. The screen opened and she read the communication.

You are cordially invited to participate in the nuptials of Zane Colton to Mirabella Freeman Colton. The ceremony will take place at Saint Luke's Parish. The virtual invitation went on to name the date.

Mirabella read the email three times just to make sure she wasn't hallucinating.

It was the same all three times.

Puzzled, confused, she pushed her chair back from her desk and went into Zane's office.

She found him sitting behind his desk, at his computer. The moment she entered, he turned his chair in her direction.

"Hi." His smile was warm and welcoming, as if he hadn't ridden in with her less than half an hour ago.

"I just got an email labeled 'For your eyes only.' What's that all about?" She wanted to know.

"It's an invitation," he told her simply. "To our wedding."

"But we're already married," she pointed out. They were, weren't they? He hadn't, for some reason, gone through a sham ceremony, hiring people to play the parts of the minister and his wife, had he?

"Yes, we are," Zane agreed, rising from behind his desk. He crossed to her. "But I thought maybe you might want to do it right, in front of your grandmother and your friends."

"Wasn't the other one legal?" she questioned.

"It was legal. It was also very small. Now that we've decided to *stay* married, I want to take vows with everyone watching so they can see for themselves that you've made me the happiest man on earth."

Her eyes sparkled, but she did her best to contain her smile. "Only on earth?"

"In the universe," he amended.

"In that case, okay," she accepted with a barely suppressed laugh. "Will there be a wedding rehearsal and everything?"

"Absolutely," he assured her. "I thought maybe we should rehearse the ending first."

"The ending?" Mirabella asked quizzically.

"Yeah, this part." Taking her into his arms, Zane offered, "Let me show you."

And, as he brought his mouth down to hers, he most certainly did.

* * * * *

16/46

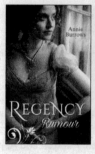

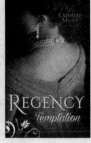